Lands of Our Ancestors
Book Three

Gary Robinson

Dedication

This book is dedicated to Native American
survivors of California's historical holocausts that
devastated Native cultures and communities
and created historical trauma for
generations of California Native Peoples.

Acknowledgments

Many thanks to Cindra Weber of the San Bernardino City Schools Indian Education Program for her support of the <u>Lands of our Ancestors</u> series and my other educational works.

Many thanks also to fourth grade teacher Dessa Drake of Templeton, California, for her enthusiasm, feedback and consultation on the series.

Additional thanks to Fred Messecar, fourth grade teacher at Rio Del Mar Elementary School in Oxnard, CA, for testing <u>Book Three</u> with his class.

Last, but not least, I say a loving thank you to my significant other, Lola, for all her love, patience and support over the past fifteen years.

Note to Teachers and Parents

This is the third and final book of the historical fiction series Lands of our Ancestors, which is the multi-generational saga of a family of California Natives who experienced several traumatic eras of California history.

What happens to the Native California characters in Lands of our Ancestors is representative of what may have happened to many of California's tribal people during the Mission Period, the Mexican Period, the Gold Rush Era, and the early years of California statehood.

The saga began in Book One with the story of Kilik, Tuhuy and the hardships their Chumash families faced during the Spanish mission era (1769-1820s).

The second book follows the main characters and their descendants into the Mexican Rancho Period in the 1820s and 1830s. This book follows this family further into the Mexican Rancho Era and then into the Gold Rush Era, and the early years of California statehood, each producing further devastation and horror for many Native peoples.

The main characters these books speak the Samala Chumash language, Spanish and one or more of the Yokuts Indian languages.

But, so you can understand what the characters are saying, you will read most of their words in English. Occasionally, Spanish or Samala words are used and appear in *italics*.

The following is a guide to the Samala Chumash words used as character names in the series, along with their meanings:

Kilik (<u>Kee</u>-leek) - Sparrow Hawk

Tuhuy (Too-<u>hooy</u>) - Rain

Salapay (<u>Sal</u>-uh-pie) - To lift or raise up

Solomol (<u>Soh</u>-loh-mole) - To straighten an arrow

Wonono (Wo-<u>no</u>-no) - Small owl

Yol (rhymes with pole) - Bluebird

Stuk (Stuke-rhymes with Luke) - Ladybug

Here are a few of the new character names found in <u>Book Three</u> that come from Samala Chumash, Coastal Chumash, Yokuts and Miwok tribal languages:

Lau-lau (*Yokuts*) - Butterfly

Taya (*Coastal Chumash* – pronounced <u>Tie</u>-ya) – Abalone

Kai-ina (Yokuts) - Woman

Alapay (*Samala Chumash* - pronounced Al-uh-pie) - Above

Malik (*Samala Chumash* - pronounced Mah-leek)
- First born child

Limik – (*Southern Yokuts* – pronounced Lee-meek) – Prairie Falcon

Tukuyun – (*Northern Yokuts* – Too-koo-<u>yoon</u>)) Jackrabbit

Tonto – (*Spanish* – pronounced Doan-doe) Stupid Fool

Loknee – (*Miwok* – Loke-nee)

Some of the Samala Chumash words, a few Yokuts words, some Spanish phrases, as well as English vocabulary words found in the book, are part of the "Words to Know" section of the <u>Book Three</u> <u>Teacher Guide</u> that is available to educators.

The guide contains an overview of the Gold Rush and Early Statehood periods, and many important elements that will help students understand this topic within the context of the California state core educational standards.

Contents

—
x

Introduction

This is a work of historical fiction based on historical facts. The characters are made up, but through them you will be able to learn things that happened to real Native Americans in California during the later years of the Mexican Rancho Period, the Gold Rush and the early years of California statehood.

You will also be able to learn more about these periods of history by reading any of the non-fiction books listed in the bibliography at the back of this book. As you read this story, ask yourself these questions.

What would you do if you had to protect your family from dangerous foreigners? How would you get them to safety and make sure they are fed and cared for? What qualities and skills would you need in order to do this? How would you react as things got worse as time went by?

These are some of the questions that our main characters, Kilik and Tuhuy, their families, and their descendants had to ask themselves as they continue on their quest of physical and cultural survival.

Characters and their Spanish Names in the Lands of our Ancestors series

Kilik (Miguel) – main character,

Tuhuy (Raphael) – Kilik's cousin

Stuk (Maria) – Kilik's younger sister

Solomol (Salvador) - Kilik's father

Salapay – Tuhuy's father

Wonono – Kilik's mother

Yol – Tuhuy's mother

Kai-ina – (Yokuts) Kilik's second wife, mother of Malik

Taya – Tuhuy's wife

Alapay (Andrea) – Tuhuy's daughter and Malik's cousin

Malik (Mateo) – Kilik's son and Andrea's cousin

Diego – Native outlaw and leader of Indians who attacked ranches

Magdalena Pacheco – Ranch owner's daughter who befriends Alapay

Limik – (Yokuts – Hawk) Kai-ina's father

Tukuyun – (Yokuts - Jackrabbit) Chief of one of the Yokuts bands

Loknee – (Miwok – Rain Falling Through) Chief of one of the Miwok bands

Mariposa – (Butterfly – Spanish) Miwok woman who marries Malik

Henry Jamieson – American newspaper reporter

3

Timeline of Events in the
Lands of our Ancestors series

1769 First Spanish mission established near San Diego

1776. Solomol is born at the Place of River Turtles

1777 Salapay is born at the Place of River Turtles

1792 Kilik is born (when Solomol is 16)

1793 Tuhuy is born

1797 Kilik's sister Stuk is born

1804 Kilik & family go to the new mission

1806 The children escape the mission Summer Solstice

The children arrive at the Place of Condors village

1811 Kilik marries Lau-lau (Yokuts) - Kilik is 19

1812 Dec. 21 - Earthquake damages missions

Kilik's unborn baby and wife die same day

1813. Stuk dies from measles brought by visitor

1814. Tuhuy leaves village to live alone

Kilik leaves village to explore

1819 Kilik returns, meets Kai-ina (Yokuts woman)

Tuhuy returns to village, sees Taya

1820 Tuhuy marries Taya -Tuhuy is 27

Simultaneous ceremony: Kilik marries Kai-ina

1821 Malik is born to Kilik & Kai-ina

Mexico wins independence from Spain

1822 Alapay is born to Tuhuy and Taya

1823 Cousins Malik and Alapay grow and play together

4

1824. Kilik begins raiding ranches and missions
for cattle - age 32

1825. Alapay blends healing and fighting as needed

1832 Kilik turns 40 years old

1833 Tuhuy turns 40 years old

1833 Kilik trains Malik as hunter & warrior

Alapay learns hunting and fighting skills

Spanish padres expelled from missions

Mission Indians released

Francisco Pacheco gets land grant - needs laborers

Epidemic flu outbreak

1834-1848. Major Mexican Rancho Period

1834 Kilik finds crippled father and aunt Yol

Pacheco's men raid Condor Village; t

Tuhuy and others taken to Ranch

Tuhuy and everyone held at ranch, must work

Kilik and Diego raid Rancho Caballero, rescue family

Kilik and family go to the Hidden Place

Village is attacked twice by Mexicans

Attackers defeated by the Native villagers

1835 Kilik and family move northward to escape

1840 Alapay and Malik spend time in the Monterey area 1846
U.S. ship sails into Monterey bay

1846-48. Mexican-American War

1848   Treaty between U.S. and Mexico signed

1849   Constitution Convention held in Monterey

1850   California accepted into U.S.

   First Governor Elected – Peter Burnett

1851   Governor Burnett declares "war of extermination" against Indians

   State legislature passes law to raise money to "exterminate Indians"

1854. California capital moved to Sacramento

1855   Catholic Church returns 11,000 acres of land to Samala Chumash People

1856. Kilik's family returns to the Place of River Turtles

Chapter One – Wearing Disguises

"The lands of our ancestors are covered with an ocean of strangers," Kilik's father had said before the family left the village known as the Hidden Place.

"Our continued survival is what's most important now," Kilik's cousin Tuhuy had added.

After Mexican soldiers and ranchers had twice attacked the village, Kilik and his family had realized they'd never be left alone as long as they lived there. So they had to move on.

As a matter of fact, all the Natives living the Hidden Place village realized they'd never again be safe there because the Mexican government that ruled Alta California knew where to find the village.

The Mexican military also knew the notorious Native American outlaws Diego and the Falcon had been hiding out there.

Diego and his followers decided to move southward to the land of the Tataviam People to escape the dangerous foreigners who had targeted Indians either for enslavement or slaughter.

However, Kilik, Tuhuy and the three generations of family with them decided to head in a northeasterly direction. Kilik's wife, Kai-ina, was from one of the tribes of Yokuts Indians. Her home village lay across the southern San Joaquin Valley in the western foothills of the Sierra Nevada Mountains. They, and Yokuts people in other villages, had somehow managed to remain mostly hidden from the Spaniards and Mexicans.

So that was their destination, a hundred-mile trek at least. This journey might require them to move in and out or through Mexican settlements, which could be very dangerous for them—unless they were disguised as Mexicans themselves.

"The best way to disguise ourselves as Mexicans is to wear their clothing," Kilik had told the others. "That means we have to take the clothes off the dead men who attacked us."

The youngest members of the family, Malik and Alapay, didn't like the sound of that at all.

"That's disgusting," thirteen-year-old Malik said with a sour look on his face. "Isn't it bad luck to touch dead people?"

"Or worse," added twelve-year-old Alapay, who looked like she might vomit. "Won't their ghosts come back to haunt us or something?"

Tuhuy was the most knowledgeable about such matters.

"Neither of those things are true," he replied. "You can put those fears out of your minds."

He thought for a moment before continuing.

"Guidance from the spirits of our ancestors told me that our continued survival is most important," he finally said. "Kilik knows better than any of us how to survive. So, as unpleasant as it may be, we need to do whatever he says, for our own protection."

Anytime Kilik and Tuhuy both agreed on something, everyone knew it must be the right thing to do. These two men, who'd led them through the worst disasters, together were like the united mind and the heart of one wise and powerful person.

After the articles of Mexican clothing had been removed, family members washed them in the river to remove stains and dirt. Then the bodies of the men were thrown in to the trenches that had previously served as part of the village defenses against attack.

Kilik's father, Solomol, had come up with the idea. He was held in the missions for a long time and held a deep resentment against the foreign invaders. He thought that burying these Spanish-speaking men in a mass, unmarked grave was fitting.

"That's how the mission priests buried our Native people when any of us died," he said. "They threw our bodies all together in one long deep trench. Spanish Catholics got individual graves with headstones and other memorial markers when *they* died, but not the Natives."

Covering the bodies with dirt and filling in the trenches had been their last task before leaving the Hidden Place.

"One last thing," Tuhuy said to his fellow travelers. "If we come across any non-Indians, remember to use your Spanish name, the one you got in the mission or the one your parents gave you. That could mean the difference between life and death."

As the eldest adult male, Solomol would normally be the one making decisions for the family and leading them on this journey. But, the older man knew very well how good his son was at every task needed for this trip.

"Tuhuy is right about Kilik," Solomol had told the family. "My son knows better than any of us how to survive these days. I, therefore, gladly yield my leadership role to him."

So for a few days now, Kilik and family had been headed in a northeasterly direction, taking back trails and old pathways, on their way across the southern portion of the San Joaquin Valley.

And what a sight they presented: a motley group of people, young and old alike, most wearing ill-fitted Mexican style clothing and carrying what few belongings they had. The only weapons they possessed, three sets of bows and arrows, were concealed inside lengths of cloth strapped to the backs of Kilik, Malik and Alapay. They were the ones best trained for combat.

But escaping detection by Mexican settlers and soldiers wasn't their only challenge. They also had to feed themselves as they traveled. Wildlife resources, both plant and animal, had already become scarce because of the intrusion of the invaders and their livestock.

Kai-ina's knowledge of her Yokuts people, the locations of their home communities and the places to find food in this unfamiliar territory is what made their journey even possible. Among other things, the Chumash had to get used to catching and cooking grasshoppers and other insects in order to survive. These were common foods to some of the Natives in these regions.

After a few hard days traveling by foot, the family camped by a small stream to eat a meager meal of toyon berries, roasted grasshoppers, bird and squirrel meat, and wild grapes.

"Many Yokuts communities are scattered along the western foothills of the Eastern Sierra Mountain range," Kai-ina told Kilik and Tuhuy. "They live almost hidden along rivers and streams that run down from those mountains."

"What's between us and those communities?" Kilik asked.

"Mostly open valley," she replied, "with very little cover to conceal us."

"What if we traveled at night and rested during the day?" Tuhuy suggested.

"That only works if there is a full moon and no clouds," his cousin replied.

"Long ago my father showed me our peoples' trails across the valley," Kai-ina said. "If we stick to those routes, we should be fine."

They all rested more easily that night knowing that there were three people—Kilik, Tuhuy *and* Kai-ina—who each had a part to play in their safe passage.

The following morning Kilik took his son aside for a father-son talk.

"There's something I've been meaning to do for some time now," he said when he was sure no one else could hear them. "I should've done it before we left the Hidden Place."

"What is it, Father?" Malik asked.

Without speaking, the Chumash warrior took the talisman necklace from around his own neck and held it out to Malik.

"Your grandfather gave this to me after I killed my first deer," Kilik said. "I was twelve years old."

Wide-eyed, Malik took the simple necklace and studied it. It was just a piece of deer antler attached to a string made of deer hide. But it had meaning far beyond the physical material it was made of.

The boy knew the necklace had been blessed by a village ceremonial leader back at the Place of River Turtles. His father had worn it every day of his life since the day he received it. It was filled with good hunting medicine, supplied by that spirit helpers that aided Solomol and the son of Solomol on every hunt.

Malik put the necklace around his own neck and suddenly felt a surge of energy pass through his body.

"Thank you, Father," the boy said reverently. "I will wear it always."

Kilik nodded his approval before they rejoined the family and continued their journey. For the next two days they followed Kai-ina as she watched the ground ahead of her. Looking for simple stone markers left by her people, she knew when to turn and when to continue in a straight line.

But on the third day, Kai-ina must've missed a marker or taken a wrong turn because the group rounded an outcropping of boulders and found themselves on a dirt road and face-to-face with a small caravan of wagons driven by Mexican merchants.

Tuhuy, Malik and Alapay rushed to the front of the line. They were the best speakers of the Spanish language because of the positions they had on Francisco Pacheco's ranch before they escaped.

14

"Hola!" Tuhuy greeted the lead wagon driver in his best Spanish. "Where are you headed?"

"Greetings, *señor*," the driver replied, eyeing Tuhuy and the others suspiciously. "We are transporting goods to the God-fearing people who've settled in the Cuyama Valley. They've been attacked by a band of dirty, filthy Indians who stole much of their food."

Tuhuy made a show of spitting on the ground as he'd seen Mexican ranch workers do when talking about Indians.

"Those filthy Indians," he said dramatically. "I spit on them!"

Satisfied with that response, the driver said, "Safe travels, my friend. May our paths cross again in the future."

With that, the man yanked on the horse reins and yelled, *"Vamonos!"*

The wagons moved on down the trail past Tuhuy and the others. Once the caravan was out of hearing range, the family exhaled a collective sigh of relief.

"That was a close call," Tuhuy's mother, Yol, said.

"Yes, but I think he was a little suspicious because none of us is wearing leather shoes," Tuhuy said.

Everyone looked down at their own foot coverings. Some wore sandals made of woven tule reads. Others wore soft, deer skin sandals.

"Unless they are among the poorest of the poor, most Mexicans do wear leather shoes," he added. "We'd better find shoes and get used to wearing them to complete our disguise."

Chapter Two – A Home Among the Yokuts

The family crossed the rest of the southern San Joaquin Valley without incident. Kai-ina eventually led them along a waterway that later became known as the Kern River. They followed its winding path up into the western foothills of the Sierra Nevada Mountains. Finally, the travelers came to Kai-ina's home village located on a small flat area that provided a view of the valley below.

"My people have lived here longer than anyone can remember," she told her husband. "The village name simply means the Place Above, because its located in the mountains. There's a spot that allows our lookouts to see to the west for miles."

A group of residents had already gathered at the edge of the village to greet them, because the lookouts had done their job. Someone was on duty day and night to prevent any of the foreign strangers from discovering their location.

At first, the scouts reported to the chief that a group of Mexicans was headed up the path, and everyone was on high alert, afraid of an attack. The group's Mexican disguises had fooled the Yokuts.

But as Kai-ina and the others got closer, one of the lookouts recognized her and canceled the warning. Fear melted into joy when the people in the village realized who was coming.

"Hello, Papa!" Kai-ina greeted her father, the village chief, whom she hadn't seen in many years. "I have missed you and Mama so much. Where is she?"

With a tear forming in the corner of one eye, the elderly man hugged his daughter, saying with sadness, "My dearest daughter, your poor mother died of a disease brought by the strangers. Several of our people became ill at the same time, but our medicine was no match for this strange illness."

Kai-ina, of course, was devastated by the news. Kilik caught her in his arms as she fell backwards, fainting with sorrow. Other members of her Yokuts family rushed to comfort her as well. Brothers, sisters, aunts, uncles and cousins she hadn't seen in years gathered around her.

After drying her eyes and gathering her strength, she made introductions all around.

"Father, this is my husband, Kilik," she said with pride. "His name means Sparrow Hawk in the Samala Chumash language."

The elder raised one eyebrow on hearing the name's meaning, and a broad smile brightened the man's face.

"My name is Limik," Kai-ina's father said. "It means Prairie Falcon in my tongue."

Then a smile also came to Kilik's face.

"That is strange and wonderful," Kilik remarked with a twinkle in his eye. "Later I must tell you of my adventures as the Falcon."

"You are the very one known as the Falcon!?" Limik said with astonishment. "Your deeds precede you. Your exploits are legendary. I do want to hear more."

Breaking in before their fascination with each other got out of hand, Kai-ina said, "And this young man is your grandson, Malik," she said.

Momentarily, Limik forgot all about the Falcon and his adventures.

"Come here, boy," the old man said. "Let me look at you."

Malik stepped forward.

"Hello, grandpa," the boy said, extending his hand. "Now I have two grandfathers in my life."

Bypassing the boy's outstretched hand, the man embraced his grandson with what could only be called a bear hug.

"Malik, does your name have a meaning?" Limik asked after ending the embrace.

"It means first born child," the boy answered.

"For me, it also means first born grandchild," the old man said. "For that is what you are to me. This is truly a wonderful day."

After everyone on both sides of Kai-ina's family had met, her father invited them all to feast with him on freshly killed deer meat. Out of respect for the eldest man in Kilik's family, Limik had Solomol up front walking with him as they made their way to the feasting area. Solomol, of course, still suffered from a broken leg that didn't heal properly so his progress was slow.

"We are hoping to stay with you, at least for a little while," Kai-ina told her father as they ate. "We are tired of being chased by the strangers and fighting with them at every turn."

"Our scouts and lookouts have reported more and more sightings of them," her father replied. "And they keep coming closer and closer to our home. The recent drought and their diseases have caused us to think about moving on ourselves."

Kilik, who understood and spoke a little of his wife's tribal language, got the gist of the old man's message and then translated it for his own father, Solomol, who didn't know the language that well.

"Where would you move to?" Kilik asked Limik. "Further east, over the mountain?"

"We considered that, but decided we'd be better off further north," he said. "If we band together with another village of Yokuts, we'll be better able to fight the foreigners if we have to. A distant relative of mine among the Foothill Yokuts said we could locate there."

After consulting with his father, Kilik asked, "May we live with you until that time? "Malik, Alapay and myself are experienced hunters and fighters. We could assist you in defending this village and feeding your people."

"I welcome you and accept your offer," the chief said. "You are now a part of my family. And when it's time to relocate, you will naturally go with us."

"Thank you," Kilik replied.

After the meal, the chief announced to his people that his son-in-law's group would be settling in the Place Above and helping in their defense if needed. That made everyone happy.

During the welcoming celebration, Tuhuy thought about all the places he, his cousin and their children had lived over the years. They were, of course, from the Chumash village known as the Place of River Turtles. When Tuhuy was eleven years old, they were forced spend some very unpleasant time at a Spanish mission. After escaping that awful place, they found their way to the village of run-aways called the Place of Condors.

While living in that village and traveling to the Sacred Mountain nearby, Tuhuy had learned how to perform an ancient ceremony called the Eyes of the Condor. After much preparation and concentration, he could see what a condor could see from up in the sky. That was helpful in finding lost people or lost things, but it didn't work every time.

A few years later, everyone but Kilik had been kidnapped from the Place of Condors by the Mexican *ranchero*, Francisco Pacheco, and forced to labor on his lands. Finally, they had been rescued by Kilik, who partnered with a Native outlaw named Diego. They had escaped to the Hidden Place but were attacked twice by Mexican soldiers.

What other attacks, disasters or catastrophes would the future bring their way? Tuhuy had never learned how to see the future, but days, months and years passed by relatively peacefully and quickly at the Place Above. Tuhuy and his family were grateful for that.

But the inevitable day finally came—the day the village elders and leaders decided it was time to move on and join another Yokuts village further north. Too many signs in the night skies had warned them of coming dangers. And too many of their sources of food and water were drying up.

Within a couple of days, Limik's people were packed and ready to leave their longtime home behind. The chief thanked the village, as if it were actually a person, for its many years of loyal service. Then he led the band of brothers, sisters and Chumash relatives down the river trail and toward a new home.

They would be traveling northward along the eastern edge of the San Joaquin Valley. Staying close to the foothills would allow them to mostly keep away from Mexican settlements or travelers. However, Kilik and his family continued to wear their Mexican disguises just in case. If one or more of the strangers came into view, Limik's people could hide while Kilik's people would converse with them in the Spanish language.

Limik's lookouts were posted at the front and the end of the line of travelers. They kept a constant watch for strangers and communicated back to the chief using a variety of animal noises to signify different things. The distinctive warble of the magpie meant all was clear. The screech of the hawk was used to signal the distant approach of one or two individuals. The wail of the coyote meant immediate danger ahead from a larger group.

On the journey, Kilik heard the distant warble of the magpie several times a day. No trouble ahead. But about three-quarters of the way to their destination, when Grandfather Sun was up in the middle of the sky, the wail of a coyote rang out. Everyone froze in place, listening whether or not the signal sounded a second time.

The coyote call came a second time, and most of the travelers scrambled for nearby bushes, trees or patches of tall grass. It was quickly decided that only Tuhuy, Malik and Alapay would remain visible to interact with whoever was coming. Kilik, Limik and three of the Yokuts warriors hid themselves nearby, arrows nocked and at the ready, if needed.

Soon five Mexican soldiers on horseback came into view, riding along a trail that came from the valley below.

"We never did find any leather shoes to wear," Alapay whispered to her father in Samala. "I hope they just think we're poor strangers."

Tuhuy shushed his daughter and whispered back, "Spanish only."

As the soldiers neared, the captain raised his fist signaling his men to stop. His long black mustache and sideburns reminded Malik of one of the vaqueros he'd worked with on Pacheco's ranch.

"Pardon the intrusion," the captain said from horseback. "Settlers in the valley reported seeing a horde of Indians walking near here. Have you seen them?"

"No, sir, we have not," Tuhuy replied. "I think we would've smelled them if they came anywhere near us."

Then, upon closer inspection, the captain noticed their dark brown skin, ill-fitting clothes and Native-looking shoes. He dismounted and approached the trio.

"Where are you coming from, and where are you going to?" he asked.

"We've come from the south, and we're headed to the north," Tuhuy replied, hoping the vague answer wasn't too suspicious sounding.

"No, I mean where *specifically* have you come from, and where *specifically* are you headed,"

"We have no real home so we must camp out and hunt for food in the wild," Tuhuy answered nervously.

"What are your names?" the captain asked, growing even more suspicious.

"I am Rafael," Tuhuy said. "This is my son, Mateo, and his cousin, Andrea."

As the five Native warriors watched from the nearby bushes, the captain took a step closer to Tuhuy. The hidden warriors quietly aimed their arrows, one at the captain's chest, the rest at the soldiers still on horseback.

"I mean what are your full names?" the captain asked, growing impatient. "You know, your first and last names."

Tuhuy faltered, fumbling for the right words to say. He'd never thought about having a last name, but he realized now that all Mexicans and Spaniards had two names like Juan Batiste or Francisco Pacheco.

"Seize them!" the captain commanded suddenly. "These three must be *Indios* disguised as Mexicans!"

The soldiers quickly jumped down from their horses as the captain drew his sword. Just as quickly, the five hidden warriors stepped out from behind their cover, drew back their bows and let their arrows fly.

Each found its mark, hitting the five soldiers squarely in their chests. Their bodies jerked backwards, falling to the ground, as cries of agony escaped their dying lips. The sudden motion and sound startled the men's horses.

"Grab the horses!" Kilik yelled in Samala. Malik and Alapy immediately sprang into action, each grasping the reins of one of the horses. Not being a man of action, Tuhuy just stood there watching, not sure what he could do.

Limik, however, understood what needed to be done. In his Yokuts language, he ordered his men to chase down the horses and bring them back. Off the men ran after the other three animals that had already headed down the hill.

Chapter Three – The Place of the Sun

Limik's men were successful at retrieving the horses, because these men were also his tribe's fastest runners. Normally they served as message carriers who ran from village to village taking important communications to the other Yokuts people.

"We can butcher these horses one-by-one," Limik said. "They'll provide food for our people a long time."

Kilik and Malik, who spoke some of the Yokuts language, immediately protested.

"They'll be more valuable to us if they are kept alive," Kilik said.

"Yes—my father, my cousin and I have all learned to ride these fine animals," Malik added. "We can use them to scout a larger area than you can on foot, and we may need them to fight if more soldiers come our way."

"But we need food!" Limik said rather forcefully. "I'm the headman of this tribe and—"

Tuhuy interrupted the man by addressing Kai-na in the Chumash language.

"Kai-ina, please tell your father I have an idea," Tuhuy said. "Ask him to hear me out."

She translated the message to her father.

The chief blew out a gust of air in frustration and, nodding his head, said, "All right, I'll listen."

"You know that Malik, Alapay and I speak the strangers' language," Tuhuy began. "I think, after removing the military saddle from one of the horses, we could take it to a nearby town and trade it for a cow."

Limik listened to his daughter's translation.

"Beef is a much better and tastier meat than horse flesh," Tuhuy added. "And we learned how to slaughter cattle on the ranch where we were forced to work."

Kai-ina finished the translation and waited for an answer.

"You are very clever people," the chief said finally. "We have much to learn from you. "You may keep three of the animals to ride."

"Thank you, Chief Limik," Kilik replied. "We honor and value your leadership."

Tuhuy and Kilik worked out a plan with Limik that would allow one of the chief's men to follow Tuhuy and Alapay toward the nearest Mexican town. The Yokuts man would hide just outside the settlement while Tuhuy and Alapay took care of the horse-cow trade.

Then he would lead the pair, with the cow trailing behind, back up into the foothills and to the Yokuts village they were all headed for. Meanwhile Malik would be in charge of the four other horses that would stay with the Natives.

Their plan went off without any problems, and by the following day, everyone safely arrived at the village where another branch of the Yokuts lived. Named the Place of the Sun, the village was known for its Summer and Winter Solstice ceremonies. It was located on a river that later became known as Kings River.

The style of homes, clothing and other details looked just like those of Kai-ina's home village.

The language, however, was slightly different, much like different Chumash communities use slightly different versions of their language.

The chief of the village was named Tukuyun, meaning Jackrabbit, because he was a fast runner as a young man. Tukuyun welcomed Limik's group with open arms, especially because they brought a cow with them. That meant a good meal for everyone there.

After the cow was butchered and cooking had begun, the older men among the travelers discussed their situation with the village chief. Kai-ina helped with the translations.

"Your ability to ride the stranger's animals *could* be very helpful to us," Tukuyun remarked. "As you said, you can scout farther from the village to watch for outsiders."

"And we can travel faster if we need to take warning messages to other nearby communities," Kilik added.

"A problem we've been facing recently is a scarcity of food resources," the chief said. "The strangers and their animals are spreading out more and beginning to wander into our tribal territories. They're either killing the wildlife or chasing it further away."

"Kilik, Malik and Alapay are excellent hunters on horseback," Solomol said. "They should be able to locate deer, elk, fox and other game animals for you."

"In exchange, you'll allow us to live here for a while?" Kilik added.

"Agreed," the chief said with a smile. "Now let's see how that cow meat is coming along over the fire."

Everyone in the village had a good satisfying meal that day, the best they'd had in quite a while. While they ate, Kilik, Tuhuy and Solomol discussed the issue of taking on Spanish surnames to help complete their disguises. Some Natives had taken the same surname as the owner of the ranch they worked at. Others had simply adopted a name that had some meanting to them.

"Each of you should select a last name that truly relates to who you are," Solomol suggested.

"Summer and winter solstice ceremonies involve the sun so I will use a Spanish last name that means "of the sun," Tuhuy said. "Solares. From now on my full Spanish name will be Rafael Solares."

"I am of the earth," Kilik said. "I have spent my life trying to protect these lands from the strangers. How would that translate into Spanish?"

"Of the earth or of the land would be De La Tierra," Tuhuy replied.

"Then De La Tierra it is," Kilik replied without further thought. "Miguel De La Tierra. But I hope to never have to use that name."

Within a few days, Kilik's extended family members all had homes to live in and tasks to take care of within the village. They settled into a peaceful pattern of daily life among the Foothill Yokuts people for several years.

Cousins Malik and Alapay spent much of their time on horseback, practicing their fighting and hunting skills. Also, they watched for any strangers that may enter their traditional territory. This activity echoed the scouting task Kilik had carried on during his teen years while living at the Place of Condors.

Even though it was dangerous, Kilik occasionally returned to his ranch-raiding practices as the Falcon in order to feed the village. Under cover of darkness, he'd sneak in to the corral of an unsuspecting *ranchero* to steal a horse, or creep into the pasture to take one of the cattle.

Kai-ina didn't like her husband taking such risks.

"Why must you continue these dangerous raids?" she asked him one time. "I'm sure we can manage to feed our families without them."

"It's not just for the food," he replied. "I can't just stand by and let those strangers get comfortable taking Native lands, enslaving Native peoples and destroying our natural world. After all these years, they're still doing it. I want them to at least pay a little for what they're doing to us."

"I know there's another reason," Kai-ina said.

"What's that?"

"You weren't meant for calm, peaceful village life," she responded. "No matter how old you get, danger and adventure are in your blood. Action is as important as the air you breathe. You probably won't settle down until you're injured or killed."

"Wife," Kilik said with a smile. "You know me too well."

Kai-ina hated to admit it, but she agreed that Kilik's mission to retaliate against the strangers was important. Someone had to mete out some justice for the wickedly cruel deeds the foreigners were committing against them.

Occasionally, also, Indians who had run away from brutal *rancheros* found their way to the Place of the Sun, and they were taken in without question.

Those Natives often reported that more strangers than ever had settled in the land, bringing with them more cattle, horses, soldiers and weapons.

And so, the pattern of their lives continued. Until…

One afternoon Malik came riding into the village at break-neck speed, calling for Kilik, Limik and Tukuyun. The three men ran to the village center as soon as they could.

"What is it, my son?" Kilik asked.

"I've seen Mexican men on horseback leading several wagons along the trail below," he said after taking a long drink of water from his water basket. "Several Native people are walking behind them, tied together by their necks, along with a few horses."

Kilik looked to Limik and Tukuyun.

"We must free those Indians and those horses," he said, and then to Malik, "How many strangers are there driving wagons or riding horses?

"About a dozen," the young man replied. "They have guns and swords, but they're not soldiers."

"It's too dangerous," Tukuyun protested. "I don't want to sacrifice any of our men."

"We have to be smart about it," Kilik replied.

He took a moment to think.

"One of the things I learned from my time with Diego is how to set a trap," he said. "I've got an idea that I know will work."

He explained the plan to the two tribal leaders.

Limik and Tukuyun talked it over and finally agreed with Kilik's strategy.

"Then we have to move quickly and quietly," the Chumash warrior said. "Have your best men gather with their weapons at the bend down river near the edge of the tree line."

Kilik explained the plan to Malik and Alapay, telling them to bring their horses to the meeting place.

Within a few minutes, horses, people and weapons had gathered at the designated place. One of the lookouts spotted the caravan on the trail. Most of the warriors took up positions just inside the edge of the tree line while three others positioned themselves behind boulders closer to the trail.

As the caravan came into view, Kilik saw that there were three wagons in the group. A half-dozen horses were tied to the second wagon, and the Indian men were tied to the last wagon.

Finally, when the procession came within range, the warriors behind the boulders stood up and shot arrows at the wagons. Then, quickly, they turned and ran uphill toward the trees.

The horseback riders drew their pistols and pursued the fleeing fighters who'd already hid behind a row of trees. There, also hidden behind trees, bushes and boulders, waited the rest of the warriors—bows, arrows and spears at the ready.

Firing their guns as they approached the tree line, the Mexican riders expected to find only the three Indians who'd shot arrows at them. Instead they found about forty armed Natives prepared to do battle.

Outnumbered, the riders turned back and fled down the hill towards the wagons. The warriors stepped from behind the trees and let their arrows and spears fly. Two of the projectiles found their marks, and two riders fell from their horses.

"*Andale! Andale!*" one of the strangers on horseback yelled at the wagon drivers. "Hurry! Let's Go."

At the same time, Kilik, Malik and Alapy slapped each of their mounts on their rumps, prompting the animals to speed after the strangers.

Bows in hand, the three chased after the Mexicans on horseback. Each time one of the strangers fired his gun back at the Indians who pursued him, an arrow flew back towards the men.

Meanwhile the lead wagon driver shouted, *"Cortar las cuerdas! Cortar la cuerdas!"* to the others with him. "Cut the ropes! Cut the ropes!"

The wagons started moving before the ropes holding the Indians were completely cut so they were dragged along the ground a few feet. Finally, their rope was severed, and the captives came to a stop in a heap. Several had been scraped and cut while being dragged.

At the same time, the horses tied to the middle wagon were allowed to run free, though they were still roped together.

"Go get those horses!" Kilik yelled to Malik and Alapay. "We need them!"

The pair headed for the freed animals at top speed.

The other Native warriors then turned their attention to the wagon drivers, hoping to cut them off from their escape route. Seeing a horde of armed Natives headed for them, most of the men abandoned their wagons and fled the scene on foot. One hid underneath the wagon he'd been driving.

The warriors immediately ceased the chase, allowing the rest of the strangers to escape, except for the two horsemen who had been killed.

Some of the Yokuts converged on the Native captives and freed them from their shackles and ropes. Speaking in one of the Yokuts dialects, the men thanked their rescuers and then started running in a group back towards their home.

Others of the men from Tukuyun's village headed for the wagons to see what cargo they carried. To their surprise and delight, the wooden crates onboard the front wagon held long and short firearms, different sizes of metal ammunition balls and leather pouches. Although none of the Natives knew how to use these items, they had all been the target of these weapons at one time or another, fired by both by Spanish and Mexican soldiers or ranchers.

The second wagon contained an assortment of supplies and equipment the Yokuts villagers weren't familiar with. This included a few burlap bags filled with a white powdery substance, cans filled with some kind of oil, and cooking pots made of hard metal.

Chapter 4 – Musket Balls and Gunpowder

Kilik approached the man cowering beneath the wagon. Not having an extensive Spanish vocabulary, the Chumash warrior used one of his arrows to tap each of the man's shoes.

"Give me your shoes," Kilik said in Samala.

"Don't kill me. Please don't kill me!" the man, who did not understand Kilik's words, replied as he curled up in a ball on the ground.

Seeing absolute fear in the man's eyes, Kilik put down his arrows and motioned towards the man's shoes. Finally, the man understood what the warrior wanted.

Hands shaking with fear, the wagon driver took off his shoes and tossed them toward the warrior.

After picking up the well-worn shoes, Kilik motioned for the man to come out of hiding. The driver didn't understand the gesture and just lay on the ground, frozen with fear.

"Come out! Come out!" Kilik yelled at the man in Samala, motioning more vigorously.

The Mexican at last got the message, and though afraid he might get an arrow in the chest, he crawled out from under the wagon.

"*Si, señor. Inmediatamente, señor.*"

Standing up and looking at his captor, the man realized he was not in immediate danger. Kilik was more interested in trying on the shoes than killing the driver. So the man thought he might be able to slip away unnoticed. He began to tiptoe his way across the rough ground.

But as one of his bare feet came into contact with a sharp rock, the Mexican yelled in pain, "*Ay!*"

Hearing the cry of pain, several other nearby warriors drew back their bows ready to shoot the stranger.

Shaking his head, Kilik waved them away.

"Don't kill him," he said. "This man is our prisoner. We will take him back to the village and try to get information from him about the strangers."

Then Kilik held up the pair of shoes for Malik and Alapay to see as they returned with the string of horses.

"Get the shoes from the fallen riders!" he called to them. "Our Mexican disguises will be complete!"

After retrieving the horsemen's shoes, Malik and Alapay brought the roped horses toward Kilik, who was still near the wagons. Kilik took charge of the captured animals and headed uphill toward the village.

Before jumping up on his own horse, Malik tied a rope around the prisoner's neck, and started leading the wagon driver toward the village like you would lead a cow.

"We'll see how you like it!" the young warrior told the Mexican as they began their journey up along the river and into the foothills. It took several of the Yokuts warriors to lead and guide the horse-drawn wagons up the narrow trail to the Place of the Sun.

Back in the village, Tukuyun tied the prisoner to a tree at the edge of the forest. While everyone else had a rare meal of venison from the deer Kilik had killed earlier, the prisoner was given dried Tule reed roots and turtle meat to eat.

A little while later, after receiving instructions from Kilik, the cousins, Alapay and Malik, approached the man. They were taking bites of venison as they talked to him.

"We'd be happy to share some of our food with you," Malik said in Spanish.

"All you have to do is answer our questions about your people," Alapay added.

"I'll tell you anything you want to know," the man quickly answered, still not convinced the Indians would let him live. "Just don't kill me."

Alapay, who had begun to develop a sixth sense about people, felt that their prisoner wasn't really a bad man. Like many of the other strangers, he was prejudiced against Indians because of ignorance and false teachings. But she decided it was best if she kept these thoughts to herself.

They led the man, who still had the rope around his neck, over to the center of the area where everyone else was eating. He was surrounded by the Native villagers, so escape was out of the question. He looked hungrily at the venison.

Tuhukyun, Limik, Solomol and Kilik looked on as Tuhuy spoke to the man in Spanish.

"You will get a bite of the meat after every question you answer," Tuhuy said.

The wagon driver nodded his agreement.

Then, in the Samala language, Tuhuy told the others, "We should find out what the man's name is."

Solomol thought for a moment, and then an idea hit him.

"When we were in the missions, the padres gave us Spanish names," the elder said. "Why don't we reverse that and give this Mexican an Indian name?

The other elders chuckled with delight at the thought.

"Let me think," Tukuyun said, casting a thoughtful gaze at nothing in particular.

"Wait, I've got an even better idea!" Solomol said. "Instead of an Indian name, let's call him the same thing the padres called us when we didn't understand what they were saying."

"What was that?" Tuhuy asked.

"Fool," the Chumash elder replied. "*Tonto*. That's one Spanish word I'll remember the rest of my life. *Tonto*. Stupid."

"That sounds good to me," Tukuyun repled. "That way, he'll understand what we are calling him instead of an Indian name he wouldn't understand. *Tonto*."

So that settled that, and the process began. Tukuyun, Limik or Kilik would ask a question in their Native tongue, which was translated by Tuhuy, Malik or Alapy. The Mexican would answer and be given a bite of venison. At first the man answered slowly and only after much thought. Soon he realized that the faster he answered, the sooner he'd receive a bite.

It wasn't long before he became very chatty, happily rambling on about life in the Mexican territory as he knew it. Among the things the Natives learned from the captive was that Monterey was the capital of the territory, and it was a wonderful place to live. Fishing boats regularly brought in fresh seafood, and ships from all over the world delivered trade goods all the time there. And there were fiestas, dances, and other exciting events to attend.

Many of the wealthier people in town had paid housekeepers and other domestic staff. Some of the nearby *ranchos* had paid jobs for workers with special skills, especially *vaqueros*. And a few of those *ranchos* even held exciting horse races that pitted riders from several other *rancheros* against each other. Huge sums of money and cattle were bet on those races.

"But it's very dangerous for *los Indios* in that area," the wagon driver added. "Tribal people from the nearby valley often raid the ranches to steal horses or cattle. So the *rancheros* and the army conduct expeditions to kill as many *Indios* as they can."

"How do you know so much about that area?" Tuhuy asked him.

"I've been driving wagons and carrying cargos between settlements for many years," he replied. "You can learn a lot if you pay attention to what's going on around you."

Leaving the man to eat the rest of his venison in peace, village leaders began discussing their captive and the information he had shared.

"What are we going to do with this man now?" Tuhuy asked. "If we turn him loose he could easily reveal our location to the Mexican army."

The older men debated the matter for a long time.

Meanwhile, all Malik could think about was the possibility of being paid for working as a *vaquero*, something he did well and really enjoyed.

Then there was also the exciting idea of racing his horse against other riders. He spoke excellent Spanish and learned much about Mexican customs while being held captive at Pacheco's *rancho*, so the thought he could easily pass for Mexican.

"Before we decide what to do with the prisoner, we will have him teach us how to use the weapons we captured," Malik's father said, interrupting the young man's day-dream. "I want you to be the first person he teaches to fire those guns, because you understand his language so well."

"Of course, Father," Malik answered.

"Then you can teach me and others here in the village," he added. "And then after that we can start teaching a few of the Yokuts warriors how to ride the horses we took."

"Sounds like a good plan," Malik said.

With Tuhuy acting as translator, Kilik made a deal with the Mexican.

"If you teach us how to load and fire the long and short guns, we'll let you go," the Chumash man said. "How does that sound?"

"Anything you want, *señor*," the Mexican replied. "Thank you, *señor*."

The training began the next day. Malik, his father and the prisoner took one of the long guns, one of the short guns, and ammo belts into the woods. Kilik and Malik both carried spears with them for their own protection.

"From now on your name is Tonto," Malik told the man once they were away from the village.

"*Oh, Dios Mio!*" the man exclaimed. "I cannot—"

Kilik placed the point of his spear against the middle of the prisoner's back.

"Was that a complaint I heard?" the warrior said in Samala.

Malik translated the question into Spanish.

"No, no, *señor*," the man immediately responded, raising his hands. "I am Tonto."

"You need to set up some kind of target against a nearby tree," the young warrior said.

"What should I use for a target?" the prisoner asked Malik who began looking around for one.

The young man zeroed in on the Mexican's wide-brimmed hat. In a surprise move, Malik grabbed the hat off his head.

"*Caramba!*" the man yelled, putting both of his hands on his head. "My hat!"

Kilik pressed the point of his spear a little harder into the middle of the prisoner's back.

"Was that another complaint I heard?" the warrior said.

"No, no, *señor*," Tonto responded, this time knowing exactly what Kilik meant. "No complaints. Not a single one."

Malik sprinted over to a tree about fifty feet away and hung the hat on a branch.

"That should work just fine," the young warrior said.

Knowing his hat would soon be shredded by bullets, the Mexican exhaled in frustration.

"Go ahead, son," Kilik said, keeping the spear point in place.

Malik picked up the long gun in one hand two different size, ball-shaped bullets in the other.

"Tonto, which size does this long gun use?"

Tonto pointed to the larger one, and Malik handed the long gun to the prisoner along with a single metal ball.

"If you point this weapon at anything but your hat, my father will ram his spear into your back," Malik whispered in the man's ear.

Tonto nodded and the warrior stepped to one side of the Mexican.

"Demonstrate how to load this weapon," Malik ordered, and the man nodded again.

"This is a front-loading musket rifle," Tonto said as hung the strap of the ammo pouch across his shoulder. "You must load the weapon with cloth-wrapped charges that contain gunpowder and a metal ball."

He then proceeded to demonstrate all the steps required to load the weapon. As he watched this complex process unfold, Kilik was thinking this took much too long. He could fire several arrows in the same amount of time. But he said nothing.

The prisoner stood up, placed the musket's wooden stock against his shoulder and pulled the gun's hammer back. Aiming for the hat on the tree branch, he squeezed the trigger. A small burst of fire shot out of the side of the gun near where the hammer came down. Simultaneously, a large burst of fire shout out of the gun's muzzle. The sound of the small explosion accompanying the fire was deafening to the ears of Kilik and his son.

Each of them yelped as the loud, sharp sound hit their ears, causing Tonto to laugh at loudly at them. The man quit laughing when Kilik glared and threatened him with the spear.

Tonto completed the lesson by demonstrating how to load and fire the short gun. It too was a muzzle-loaded weapon and used the same process as the musket.

"This pistol can be loaded and fired more quickly than the long musket, but it is less accurate," he said.

"I remember a Spanish soldier firing one of these at me when I was a teenager," Kilik said. "Thankfully he missed."

After loading and firing the weapon two more times, he handed the gun to Malik.

"Now you try it," Tonto said.

The young warrior took the gun and copied the steps Tonto had taken. After the ammunition had been loaded, Malik aimed at the hat. Before squeezing the trigger, he closed his eyes and put one hand over the ear closest to the weapon. He fired, then opened his eyes.

"You missed because you weren't aiming at the target, and you looked like a little boy while firing," Tonto said. "Try again, and this time fire the gun like a man."

Malik tried it one more time, standing tall, eyes open, ears uncovered. He managed to keep from squinting as he pulled the trigger, and the bullet hit the hat dead center. Malik ran over to the hat, plucked it off the branch and brought it back for his father to examine.

"Outstanding!" Kilik exclaimed. "I knew you could do it."

Afterwards they led Tonto back to the village where Malik tied him up to a tree while Kilik went to report the success of the firearm training session to the elders. Alapay came over as her cousin finished tying the man up.

Chapter 5 – The Monterey Plan

"Now you can release me, right?" Tonto said excitedly. "I have done as you asked."

Ignoring Tonto's question, Alapy asked Malik in Samala, "How did the weapon lessons go? I heard the shots."

"You said you'd release me," Tonto interjected, not understanding what the cousins were saying.

"It was good," Malik replied to Alapay, again ignoring the prisoner. Then, changing the subject, he asked her, "Are you ready to have that talk with our fathers?"

Now, almost begging, Tonto said, "Please release me, *señor*. I have done as you asked."

"Ready as I'll ever be," Alapay confirmed. "Let's go do it."

They left Tonto and headed to the center of the village to speak to Tuhuy and Kilik.

"Why don't you answer me?" Tonto called after them, but they still ignored him.

With Alapay by his side, Malik started the conversation with their fathers.

"When it's time to let our prisoner go, we want to take him to Monterey and release him," he said. "Then we'll both stay in the area to learn more about the strangers."

"Why would you want to do that?" Malik's father asked in a state of shock.

"The truth is I loved working as a *vaquero*, and Tonto said there are ranches that will pay me to do that work," Kilik's son answered. "I have all the skills needed, the Mexican clothes, and knowledge of the language and the customs of the Mexicans. I could fit right in."

"But you'd be working for our enemies!" Tuhuy protested.

Alapay stepped forward.

"These people aren't all bad, Father," she said. "But whatever we think of them, they're here to stay. The sooner we accept it and adapt, the better off we'll be. Before we left

56

the Hidden Place, you yourself said we must find ways to blend in to survive."

Tuhuy just shook his head as he thought back to those days.

"I can't believe my own son and niece are saying these things to me!" Kilik replied.

"Here's the idea I have," Malik said. "On the ranch I can listen as the strangers talk among themselves and find out if anyone is planning one of their attacks on us or our neighbor tribes. Also, I may be able to 'accidentally' allow a few of the horses or cattle to escape. That will make them easy for you or other Natives to capture."

After hearing this unexpected proposal, Tuhuy and Kilik went off to talk it over. The older cousins spent a few minutes of heated debate and then returned to the younger cousins with an answer.

"We decided to let you two carry out this unusual plan—under one condition," Tuhuy said.

"What's that?" his daughter asked.

"That you both promise to immediately leave the town or the ranch to ride here and warn us of any impending attack," Kilik answered.

"Of course, Father," Malik said. "No question about it."

Speaking to his daughter, Tuhuy asked, "And what do you plan on doing in Monterey?"

"Find paid work as a domestic," she replied. "And I hope to learn to read and write the strangers' language. Who knows, it might come in useful one day."

"Fine—Now, all we have to do is convince both of your mothers this is a good idea," Kilik said with a sigh.

As the two men walked away to talk to their wives, Malik and Alapay headed for the prisoner.

"Okay, here's the plan," Malik told Tonto. "First we will teach a few of the warriors here how to use the weapons and ride the horses we captured so they can protect themselves from your people. Then my cousin and I will personally take you to Monterey and set you free."

"*Ay Caramba!*" the man exclaimed. "That's wonderful news."

It took about two weeks to train a handful of Yokuts warriors to ride and care for the horses, as well as train them to load and shoot the Mexican weapons. It took Tuhuy and Kilik almost that long to convince their wives to let the two cousins travel to, and settle in, enemy territory.

It wasn't long before Malik and Alapay were ready to embark on the journey to Monterey that would begin the next chapter of their lives. At gunpoint and under protest, Tonto was forced to remove his clothing and replace it with a deer hide shirt and loincloth. Also at gunpoint, the man was forced to mount his horse. His hands were then tied to the saddle horn.

"Oh, Dios Mio!" the man uttered under his breath.

Wearing their Mexican clothes, Malik and Alapay made their tearful goodbyes and mounted their horses. With bags of dried foods for the trip, off the unusual looking trio went.

Along the way, the cousins talked about their situation and discussed some options for the future. The year was 1840, and Malik was nineteen years old, anxious to explore more of the territory and strike out on his own. Action is what he craved, just like his father. He loved his parents but wanted to make his own decisions in this rapidly changing world.

Alapay, only eighteen, had some of the same desires. She was a unique young woman, having been trained to fight, hunt and ride as no other Native girl had.

But she had inherited spiritual gifts and sensitivities from her father as well, and these traits allowed her to perceive things that other people didn't.

Sure, she had loved using her intuitive healing powers to cure her indigenous relatives and friends of their ailments. But traditional Native culture could put limitations on a young woman. Because of the two main influences in her life, Kilik and Tuhuy, she was a thinker and a doer. She wanted to experience more of the world around her, even if parts of that world were dangerous and unfamiliar.

Three long days of travel brought the threesome to the edge of Monterey, a bustling Mexican town sitting right on the Pacific Ocean. With Malik in the lead, they proceeded to the center of town and carried out the planned release of their prisoner.

Tonto, of course, had been dressed up as a Native American for the trip. With a gag in his mouth, he had been tied to the saddle of a horse and led across the valley and into town.

When they arrived at the center of town, Malik removed the man's gag and slapped his horse on the rump. The animal sped away. At the same time, the two Natives began yelling in Spanish, "*Ese Indio se escapó!* That Indian escaped! Somebody, get him!"

As the horse ran through the street, Tonto yelled, "I am not an Indian. I am Mexican. Someone help me!"

Malik and Alapay laughed and laughed as they watched the horse and rider create such a hilarious scene on the streets of Monterey. They figured someone would probably capture him and haul him off to a ranch to work until he convinced them he wasn't Native.

The two cousins never did find out what happened to Tonto after that.

Back at the Place of the Sun, the warriors continued practicing with the guns by taking them on hunting trips. The long rifles proved so effective that they quit using their bows all together. That is, until they ran out of gunpowder. With no means of obtaining more of the explosive material, the guns became useless. All that remained were a few pouches filled with the small lead balls hurled by the gunpowder.

Chapter 6 – Mateo and Andrea

Alapay and Malik wandered around Monterey for a couple of hours, marveling at the hustle and bustle of the busy town and the large ships docked in the harbor. Posted on the side walls of buildings and lampposts all over town were printed signs with Spanish lettering. People stopped to look at them and talk about what was there. Since neither of the cousins could read the language, they had no idea what was on those signs.

The two Indians were unaware that this city was the capital of Alta California and that many important decisions were made here.

What they <u>were</u> aware of was that they didn't know how to find a place to stay, food to eat, or jobs that paid them the cash they needed to survive in the Mexican society. Fortunately, they did speak the language.

"I will start talking to people to see if anyone needs a house maid," Alapay said. "I know I can do that job since that's what I did at *Ranchos Caballeros*."

"And I'll start asking people how to get to the nearest ranches," Malik replied. "That's where the *vaquero* jobs are."

With those plans in mind the cousins split up, promising to meet at the spot where they now stood at the end of the day.

Malik asked several men on the street where the nearest ranches were or if they knew of any *vaquero* jobs in the area. Each named one or two possibilities. After mounting his horse, the young man rode out of town on a different road than the one they'd come in on to find those ranches.

Meanwhile, Alapay asked several women on the street if they knew of any housekeeping jobs in the area. Again, each one named one or two possibilities. After mounting her horse, the young woman started looking for the locations that had been described to her.

By the time the sun was about to set, neither of them had found a job. They returned to their meeting place right at sundown. Each reported their lack of progress, so they decided to ride out to the edge of town to camp for the night.

They easily located a tree-covered hill overlooking the seaport town and the bay. A few lights flickered in some of the homes and buildings below. They spent a peaceful night there.

The following morning, the pair awoke to a bright sunrise.

"Today's the day something good is going to happen," Alapay said, rubbing the sleep from her eyes. "Last night I dreamed I found a long-lost friend."

"Who was it?" Malik asked after a big yawn.

"I never got to see her face, but somehow I knew it was a friend who would help me," his cousin replied.

"All right, I guess we'll see."

They ate the remaining food they'd brought with them, and then Malik suggested they again connect at sundown at their original meeting place in town.

"If you find work at a ranch, how will you be able to let me know where you are?" Alapay asked. "You may not be able to come back into town."

"Oh, I hadn't thought of that," Malik replied. "I'll find a way to get to you, if not today, then tomorrow."

Alapay didn't feel confident in that plan but agreed with her cousin anyway. Again, they went their separate ways. The young woman went into the center of town and searched for a large two-story house just a few blocks from the water front. The day before, a very nice Mexican woman had said that the owner, Señor Larkin, was looking for additional household staff. The woman also said the man was *Inglés*—English.

Alapay had never heard the word "English" before, but that didn't really matter. There was the possibility of job in that house. Starting at the boat docks, she worked her way back and forth on the nearby streets. After about a half-hour, she rounded a corner and easily spotted what she was looking for: the largest house in the neighborhood. Once Alapay had tied her horse to the railing in front of the place, she knocked on the front door.

That's when she remembered she would have to go back to calling herself Andrea. That's the Spanish name her father had chosen for her when she was born. The name had served her well while she lived and worked at *Ranchos Caballeros* as a young teen.

After a short wait, a young woman about Andrea's same age opened the door. To hes surprise and delight, there stood her old friend Magdalena, daughter of *ranchero* Francisco Pacheco.

"Andrea?" the young Mexican woman said with shock on her face.

"Magdalena?" the young Native woman said, equally shocked.

Magdalena pulled her long-lost friend in for a hug, and the pair held their embrace for several minutes.

"What are you doing here?" Magdalena asked, finally pulling away. "I thought I'd never see you again."

"I heard there was a job for a housekeeper here," Andrea replied. "What are you doing here?"

"Long story," Magdalena answered. "I'll tell you all about it later. But first, let's get you settled in here. You're hired!"

Magdalena, who served as the head of the Larkin household staff, showed Andrea around the two-story house. Actually, it was a mansion when compared to other homes in the area.

"The owner, Mr. Larkin, is an American who moved here a few years ago," the head housekeeper explained. "He's a very nice man."

"What's an American?" Andrea asked.

"Many English-speaking people who lived in the United States have settled in Monterey," Magdalena said. "They are called Americans. Their population is growing quickly."

After the tour, Andrea was shown to her sleeping quarters, a small but nice room on the first floor near the kitchen. Magdalena brought her some clean clothes, which was a uniform all the staff wore.

"In addition to your own room, you'll receive food, clothing and a small salary while working here," Magdalena said. "I have to finish a chore in the back of the house so you make yourself comfortable until I get back. We have a lot to catch up on."

As her friend headed off down the hall, Andrea had a feeling she was going to really like it there. Later in the day, she was introduced to Mr. and Mrs. Larkin. As she stood near the couple, Andrea sensed what these people were like. The husband was keeping some sort of big secret, a secret that had to do with him being an American in Mexican territory. His wife, also an American, had no such secrets. She busied herself with raising their son and running the household.

Meanwhile, Malik had ridden his horse in an eastward direction along a narrow dirt road. He'd heard about a ranch called *Rancho Buena Vista* about twenty miles away from Monterey. If the information was correct, they needed to hire a half-dozen *vaqueros* to help with a large number of cattle the *ranchero* had purchased from another ranch.

Arriving at the ranch, Malik located the foreman and asked about a *vaquero* job. The older man, named Vicente, confirmed that he was hiring and asked the young man to demonstrate his cowboy skills. Malik was happy to show Vicente his ability to cut a particular calf from the herd, lasso the animal, wrestle it to the ground and mark it with the ranch's brand.

Seeing the musket-style pistol the young man carried, Vicente said he'd like to see a shooting demonstration as well. The foreman led Malik to another part of the ranch.

"This is where we regularly hold target practice," Vicente said.

He pointed across an open area to three targets standing about one hundred feet away. A feeling of dread coursed through Malik's body when he saw the targets.

They were crude wooden cutouts of California Indian men, complete with faces, bodies, arms and legs. The targets were riddled with bullet-holes.

"I'd like to see you hit that middle target in the head or chest," Vicente said.

Malik just stood there for a long minute, unable to move.

"Go ahead, I'm waiting," the foreman said.

Malik took a deep breath, pulled his gun from his belt and fired. The bullet hit the wooden Indian in the middle of the head.

"Yahoo!" Vicente yelled. "Another one bites the dust!"

Expressionless, Malik stuck the gun back in his belt and let out a deep breath. He hoped he wouldn't be expected to do that with a real Native person.

The foreman was so impressed with the young man's skills, speed and accuracy with a firearm, he offered him the job right there on the spot. Malik now wasn't so sure he still wanted the job. But he decided that his role as spy for his village was a most important job, so he pretended to be very happy.

Malik had introduced himself as Mateo De La Tierra, the full Spanish name his family had started using.

This ranch, owned by *Señor Estrada*, was smaller than Pacheco's place, but there was plenty of room to run a large herd of cattle.

He was given a bed in the cowboy's bunk house for sleeping and was promised meals and a salary to be paid at the end of each month. After meeting some of the other cowboys, the young Native man felt okay being there, even though he was surrounded by men who might enslave or murder him if they knew he was an *Indio*.

Each of the two Native cousins fell into familiar daily patterns similar to those they'd experienced at *Rancho Caballeros,* except this time they received much better treatment and much better food.

Mr. Larkin, who spoke and read both English and Spanish, was well known in the Monterey community. He operated a store out of one end of his home so his place became a crossroads of information, news, ideas and social activity. Magdalena was learning to speak and read English from her employer, skills she promised to eventually share with Andrea.

Mateo fit in quite well with the other cowboys at the ranch but was worried about how he was going to let his cousin know where he was.

At sunset, Andrea went to the meeting place in hopes of seeing Mateo, but her cousin never came. For the next week she continued showing up at the spot near sunset, but it was the same each day—no Mateo.

"Creator, take care of my cousin," she whispered in a prayer. "We <u>must</u> find each other again soon."

She already missed him and the rest of her family, but this was the choice she had made so she was going to stick with it.

Back at Tukuyun's village, the family continued with their lives, or at least tried to. Kilik's father, Solomol, and Tuhuy's mother, Yol, were feeling their age. Both of the sixty-four-year-olds had begun to experience the aches, pains and ailments that often plague elders. Tuhuy had treated the two oldest members of their family as best he could with medicinal herbs and traditional healing skills.

One evening Yol and Solomol sat together near a warming fire to discuss their troubled pasts and their uncertain futures.

"Yol, can you remember our days back at the Place of River Turtles when our children were young and life was simple?" Solomol asked his sister-in-law.

"I remember many of those times with great fondness," she replied. "But those memories are fading like a night time dream fades when you awake in the morning. I have to reach deep within my memory to try and revive them."

"I haven't spoken to anyone else in the family of this," Solomol said. "But I would dearly love to see our home one more time before I die. Do you think that's possible?"

"Is what possible?" a voice from behind them asked.

Turning around, they saw Tuhuy approaching. Solomol repeated the question for his nephew.

"That's a hard question to answer," Tuhuy replied. "We really don't know what has been happening there since we came north. The strangers have taken over much of the lands that were once ours to run their cattle, build their towns and plant their crops."

"Son, would you be able to use the Eyes of the Condor ceremony to see what has become of our homeland?" Yol asked, knowing that Tuhuy had received the gift of spiritual vision many years ago.

"I can try, Mother, though it has been a long time since I've done the ritual and called on that gift," he replied. "It will take some practice, but I will try."

Chapter 7 – The Cowboy and the Maid

In Monterey, the months passed quickly for Andrea. True to her word, Magdalena spent time each day teaching her to read Spanish. So, when she strolled around town or ran errands for Mr. Larkin, she could begin to read all those printed paper signs stuck to walls and lampposts.

For Mateo, time traveled more slowly as he worked on the ranch. He <u>did</u> enjoy the daily activities of cowboy life, but he didn't realize the experience would be so lonely for him. He, too, missed his cousin and the rest of his family.

That is until he caught sight of a beautiful young Native woman who was one of the unpaid works there.

He would see her coming out of the main house at the same time every day bringing food scraps to feed the ranch's chickens. But he had to be careful, because it was forbidden for Mexican ranch hands to interact with the captive Native women.

One day he got up the courage to speak to her, and he hid himself around the corner behind the barn next to the chicken coops.

"What is your name?" he asked her in Spanish as she came around the corner.

This startled the young woman, causing her to drop her basket of food.

"Oh, you scared me, *señor*!" she exclaimed.

She looked up at him as she stooped to retrieve the basket and its contents. Noticing that he wore the outfit of a vaquero, she added, "You really should not be talking to me, you know. It's against the rules for a Mexican man to be talking to a Native woman here."

"I won't tell, if you won't," he whispered, stooping down to help her. "If you promise to keep a secret, I'll tell you who I really am."

She stopped what she was doing and looked directly into his eyes.

"I promise."

"First you have to tell me your name," he requested.

"Mariposa," she answered, a Spanish name that meant Butterfly.

Mateo was surprised and pleased with her answer. Mateo's father had told him of his first wife who was named Butterfly in the Yokuts language. She had died, along with her unborn baby, on a strange and fateful night many years ago when Mother Earth shook beneath their feet.

"Perfect," he said. "I am actually an Indian of Chumash and Yokuts blood, disguised as a Mexican. But, of course, you can't tell anyone."

Again, she was surprised by his words.

"What is your name?" she asked.

"Mateo De La Tierra is my Spanish name," he replied. "Malik is my Indian name. Do you have a name in your Native language?"

"Sadly, no," she answered. "I was born and raised in Mission San Jose and given only a Spanish name at birth. Many of my Miwok people were stolen by soldiers and brought to the mission to work."

"Mariposa is a beautiful name, just like you," Mateo said.

The young woman blushed.

"Where do your Miwok people live?" the young man asked.

"Oh, it is the most beautiful place north of here among the marshes and tributaries of the great river that flows from the ocean into our valley," she said with a fondness in her voice. "But I have only seen my people's homeland twice in my life."

"Maybe we can go there together some day," Mateo offered.

Then they heard footsteps headed their way.

"Meet me at midnight, if you can, at the horse barn so we can talk without being discovered," he whispered.

"I will try," she said as she hurried to feed the chickens.

That night she sneaked out of the Native sleeping quarters to meet Mateo. Under a full moon and a sky filled with stars, the couple got to know each other. And for several nights in a row, they secretly met and continued to grow closer little by little.

By day, when he wasn't out herding cattle or mending fences, he'd position himself so she'd pass by him on her way to the chicken coops. They just smiled at one another as she passed.

Back in Monterey, Andrea was noticing that more and more English-speaking people were arriving in town. Magdalena said they were showing up in Alta California at an alarming rate.

"One day soon, they may outnumber us," Magdalena commented.

Andrea remembered that several times over the years her father and uncle remarked that strangers, first Spaniards and then Mexicans, were moving into the lands of their ancestors at an alarming rate. Now the strangers were beginning to experience that feeling themselves.

Unlike her cousin, Andrea had not been attracted to any one she met in her daily life. Maybe it was because, other than Magdalena, these people regularly displayed their prejudice against Indians. Thanks to Andrea's continuing explanation of Native American culture, Magdalena came to understand the Indian point of view and appreciate their cultures.

"Are you going to tell me how you ended up here?" Andrea asked her friend after one of their discussions. "Why did you leave *Ranchos Caballeros*?"

"After you and your people escaped, my father became a bitter man," Magdalena answered. "I mean, he was already a harsh person, but his mood turned dark and unforgiving."

"That's too bad," Andrea commented.

"I couldn't stand to be around him so I packed a few of my things, threw them in a carriage and came here," Magdalena continued. "I was lucky to come across Mr. Larkin just as he finished building this house."

"Creator helped you find him and then helped me find you," Andrea said.

As the days went by, Magdalena began to teach Andrea how to say a few English phrases and to recognize a few of those phrases when written. The Native woman was a fast learner.

But Andrea began to notice a difference in herself as she continued living in this busy seaport away from natural surroundings. Her spiritual sensitivity seemed to be decreasing. Her healing gifts were suffering, maybe because she could no longer draw energy from the spirits of the natural world. Or maybe it was because she was surrounded by the strangers whose own spirits were not focused on living in harmony with nature.

This was a concern that began to nag at her as time passed, but she pushed it aside temporarily.

Then one Monday, the two of them walked together to the fish market to purchase items for the evening dinner. On the way they came across a printed paper sign affixed to the side of the customs house. It announced a coming event that featured a horse race between the fastest riders from nearby ranches. The news excited Andrea.

"Maybe my cousin Mateo will be among the riders!" she told her friend excitedly. "He always wanted to be in a horse race! Can we go?"

Reading the date of the race posted on the sign, Magdalena replied, "It's happening this Sunday, our day off, so we can certainly go."

When Sunday finally arrived, the two friends walked the few blocks to the open field at the edge of town where the race would take place. Hundreds of other people had the same idea. Crowds of people lined both sides of the race course. Near the finish line, men dressed in their finest Sunday clothes placed bets on the race and received tickets that recorded their wagers.

Andrea searched for an area where the horses and their riders were gathered near the starting line. She located it close to a grove of oak trees at the far end of the field.

"I'm going to look for my cousin," she told Magdalena.

"I'll find us a place to watch the race," her friend replied.

Reaching the grove of trees, Andrea searched the faces of the riders. Finally, she saw Mateo cinching up the saddle on his horse and rushed over to him. Not having heard from him for months, she was so relieved that he was alive and well. But in her excitement, she forgot to call him by his Spanish name.

"Malik, Malik, I am so happy to see you!" she yelled as she approached.

"Shhhhh!" Mateo replied in a loud whisper as she hugged him. "Do you want people to find out who we really are?"

"Oops," she grimaced. Then louder, "Mateo, how have you been?"

Leading his horse, he moved them further from the other riders.

"I'm at *Rancho Buena Vista* east of here," he said. "But I may not be able to stay there long."

"Why?" his cousin asked, "What's going on?"

"Indians from the valley have been stealing more and more horses and cattle," he answered. "There's talk of sending expeditions to attack them. I'm afraid my father might be among those doing the stealing."

"I am living and working in town at the home of a wealthy man named Mr. Larkin," Andrea said.

She told him that she'd found her long-lost friend, Magdalena, and how wonderfully things were going.

"If you need to find me that's where I'll be," Andrea concluded. "Everyone in town knows the place."

Just then the call went out for riders in the first race to mount up and head to the starting line.

"I have to go now," Mateo said as he mounted his horse. "I probably won't see you after the race, but you can ask anyone how to get to the ranch if you need me."

He rode towards the starting line, leaving Andrea feeling cheated out of the time she hoped to spend with her cousin. They had been through so much together, and she was missing him. In fact, her heart ached at being away from the rest of her family for so long.

Andrea joined Magdalena just in time to see the race start. A dozen horses bolted from the starting line and headed across the flat field at top speed. Andrea didn't understand why Mateo started out lagging a little behind the main cluster of racers. Then she saw the leaders of the pack jockeying for the front position. The riders pushed and shoved each other trying to move ahead.

Suddenly, two riders fell from their horses and were immediately trampled. The crowd reacted with loud gasps, and Andrea saw the wisdom of her cousin's strategy. Now he gently whipped his steed on the rump, and the animal shifted into high gear. Coming up from the outside of the tightly clustered pack of horses, Mateo overtook the lead horse and crossed the finish line a full length ahead of the others.

Many people in the crowd cheered while the men who'd bet heavily against *Rancho Buena Vista* threw their betting tickets angrily on the ground. Andrea watched as her cousin rode his winning horse to an area in front of the crowd of spectators.

A man, who must have been the owner of the ranch and Mateo's boss, stood next to him proudly. The short, chubby man hoisted a bag of gold and silver coins up in the air. This was the money he'd just won from the other ranch owners who had placed bets on the first race.

The *ranchero* reached in the bag a removed a handful of the coins and gave them to Mateo. Beaming with pride, Mateo scanned the crowd looking for Andrea. He winked at her when he finally spotted her and displayed the handful of coins.

Chapter 8 – The Falcon Rides Again

Mateo had been right about his father. Kilik <u>was</u> one of the
Natives leading raids on Mexican ranches to steal horses and
cattle. The Falcon had risen again. His people were hungry,
and he was angry at the strangers. They were spreading out
further and further across the countryside, gobbling up prime
ancestral hunting and food gathering lands.

Printed posters started showing up on the ranches of
the region and on the walls and signposts in Monterey. They
said, "Wanted Dead or Alive—The Indian Outlaw known as
The Falcon." Of course, none of the Mexican citizenry knew
what he looked like. They just knew he must be captured or
otherwise stopped.

But the Falcon was getting older. His mind and body weren't as agile as they used to be. His arrows didn't always hit their marks like they once did. His horsemanship skills began to decline as well.

This became painfully apparent on one particular raid. Kilik led four other Native horsemen further westward than they'd ever traveled before, because *rancheros* close to their village had started protecting their herds by posting armed guards twenty-four hours a day.

In the early morning hours before dawn, the four approached a ranch they hadn't previously raided. The Indian outlaw didn't know this was the very ranch where his son worked as a *vaquero*.

A set of brands had been burned into posts and trees that stood at the property's edge, but no fence enclosed the land. Kilik scanned the horizon until he spotted a column of smoke rising straight into the sky. He knew the smoke was coming from the main ranch house and headed in that direction.

Soon the Natives saw the horse corral surrounded by a wood railing fence next to a barn. At a signal from Kilik, the four Native horsemen slapped their steeds into full speed. The plan was to head straight for the corral, open the gate and get away with a few head of the best stock.

However, before the riders got very close, two vaqueros unexpectedly stepped out from behind the barn. One man began loudly ringing a nearby bell, sounding an alarm to awaken the other cowboys. Within a matter of minutes, more cowboys with guns had shown up on the scene. One of those was none other than Kilik's own son, Mateo. The young man knew he was expected to fire his weapon at the Native horse thieves but never planned to do so. The *vaquero* standing beside him took aim at the lead rider, who looked familiar to Mateo. Just as the man fired his weapon, the young man recognized the rider as his father.

Hearing the sound of the shot, Kilik avoided being hit by ducking his head and sliding sideways on the horse. Without skipping a beat, the horses of all four riders then made abrupt turns outside the corral and began to retreat.

Mateo aimed his pistol slightly off target and pulled his trigger. The bullet whizzed harmlessly over the riders' heads. However, another cowboy's bullet clipped the last rider, knocking him to the ground. Kilik looked back in time to see that rider fall and then caught sight of his son among the cowboys.

Another bullet from a different cowboy's gun sped through the air, hitting the lead rider in the left shoulder. Mateo saw his father slump over on this horse. The young man accidentally let out a yelp on seeing blood spurting from the wound. Quickly, he covered his mouth.

While the other cowboys rushed over to the fallen Indian to see if he was still alive, Mateo continued to watch his father escape in the distance.

The Native who'd fallen from his horse struggled to stand up. He, too, had been hit in the shoulder. Pulling a pistol from his waistband, the ranch foreman shot the man dead. Sadly, Mateo recognized his fallen brother as one of the village men he'd help train to ride and shoot. But, of course, he couldn't say or do anything about it.

Gazing off in the direction his father had ridden, Mateo prayed to Creator that his father would be all right. The young man knew then that he'd made a foolish choice to come work for the strangers who thought of Indians only as work animals.

Raids like the one Mateo had just witnessed prompted Mexican militias to conduct frequent raids to punish the Indians for stealing their livestock.

The men who conducted these unofficial expeditions didn't waste time trying to find out who was guilty and who was innocent. They slaughtered any Natives in the wild they came across.

News of these raids reached Andrea and Magdalena in Monterey and both were disturbed by what they heard. Little did either of them know of the turmoil that was about to engulf them and disturb their lives even more. With too few soldiers to maintain security, weak leadership within the government, and an inpouring of American immigrants, Mexico was losing control of its citizens and its territory.

In 1846, an American ship sailed into Monterey Bay, raised the American flag over the customs house and claimed the territory on behalf of the United States. This action met with no resistance from the people of the city. Later that year, California's first newspaper, *The Californian,* was printed in Monterey, half in Spanish and half in English. Thanks to Mr. Larkin, Andrea and Magdalena could read both halves of that paper. From its pages, the young women learned that the Mexican-American War had begun.

"Do you think they'll be fighting in the streets of Monterey?" Andrea asked her friend.

"Mr. Larkin said that the United States is hungry for all the lands from here to a place called Texas," Magdalena answered. "He thinks the battles will mostly happen in other places, so we should be all right here."

But twenty miles east of town, Mateo was hearing a different kind of disturbing news. Ranch owners from several nearby ranches had come to *Rancho Buena Vista* for a meeting. Several of the cowboys, including Mateo, stood near a window just outside of the room where the meeting was taking place. They heard every word of that gathering.

"I'm sick and tired of losing my horses and cattle to those dirty, thieving Indians!" one *ranchero* exclaimed. "They've got to be punished severely and soon."

"If we pool all our horses, men and guns, we can ride over to the valley and start wiping them off the face of the earth!" another man shouted.

"Let's take a vote," a third man said. "All those in favor of this action, say aye."

Every man in that room shouted, "Aye!"

"All opposed say no."

The room was silent.

"Then we shall mount an expedition against the savages," the owner of *Rancho Buena Vista* said. "Have your men ready to ride in three days."

The *vaqueros* that stood near Mateo cheered with excitement at the decision.

"We'll kill 'em all, big and small!" one of them said.

"Those filthy heathens won't know what hit 'em," another one remarked.

Mateo, on the other hand, went into a panic. His mind swirled in a state of confusion as he tried the think what he must do. He had to warn his family and the others in Tukuyun's village.

Quickly, he dashed to the bunk house to gather up what few belongings he had. Then he went to the stables and saddled up two horses. Lastly, he went to find Mariposa. She happened to be on her daily trip to the chicken coops. Mateo waited in his usual spot for her and startled her as she came around the corner of the barn.

"Mariposa, I have to speak to you," he said in a loud whisper.

"Mateo, you frightened me," she said holding her hand over her heart.

"I'm sorry, but this is an emergency," he said. "*Señor Estrada* and the other ranch owners are going to attack the Native villages in the valley east of here. They plan on killing any Indians they see."

"That's terrible," Mariposa said. "What are you going to do?"

"I have to go warn my family and help protect them," he answered. "I want you to come with me."

"Me, go with you?"

"Yes, I have a horse all saddled and ready for you to ride," he said. "We have to go now!"

She hesitated, looking from him to the main ranch house where she worked.

"I love you and want to marry you, Mariposa!" Mateo added urgently.

"That's all I needed to hear," she said enthusiastically. "What are we waiting for?"

With a broad smile on his face, Mateo took his beloved by the hand and led her to the stables. Before mounting their horses, the young man asked, "Have you ever ridden horseback before?"

"Only almost every day as a young girl," Mariposa replied. "At the mission my father was a *vaquero* and he taught me to ride."

"Perfect!" Mateo said as he helped her up on her horse. "First we must ride to Monterey so I can tell my cousin what's going on. Then we'll turn around and head east to the village where the rest of my family lives."

"I am with you all the way," she replied, and the couple rode out of the ranch at top speed.

Andrea was very surprised to see her cousin at Mr. Larkin's front door. After a quick introduction to Mariposa, Mateo launched into his explanation of why he was there and what they needed to do. His cousin was at first reluctant to leave her friend and her comfortable life.

"You can stay if you want, but I think we've been living in a fantasy world among the strangers," he said, speaking the Samala language in a heated tone. "We belong back with our people carrying on our family's traditions and defending them from attack!"

Andrea only hesitated a moment longer before replying.

"Come around to the back of the house to the stables while I tell Magdalena what's going on," she said finally. "Then I'll saddle my horse, and we'll be on our way."

Mateo and Mariposa waited near the back stables for only a short while before Andrea and Magdalena emerged from the back of the house. Mateo's cousin began saddling her horse.

"You are right to come fetch your cousin so you can both go and protect your family," Magdalena told Mateo. "My people are really the barbaric ones for treating your people the way they do. I wish you all a safe journey."

Mateo thanked her for her concern as he and Mariposa mounted their horses. With a tear in her eye, Andrea gave her Mexican friend a long goodbye hug. After mounting her own horse, Andrea called to Magdalena, "May our paths cross again one day. Goodbye for now, sister!"

The three Natives rode away from Monterey as Alapay wondered if their paths really ever would cross again. As they rode east, Malik told his cousin about the Indian raid on *Rancho Buena Vista* when one of the members of their village had been killed and his father wounded.

Chapter 9 – New Rulers, New Laws

Back in Tukuyun's village, life as the people knew it came to a halt as Malik, Mariposa and Alapay rode in that day. Lookouts had already seen the three coming and alerted the people to gather. Limik, Solomol, Tuhuy and Tukuyun waited at the front of the crowd.

"We bring bad news from the Mexican ranches!" Malik told the tribal leaders as he dismounted.

"They will attack us and all the Indians in the region within two or three days!" Alapay added. "We must abandon the village immediately."

"Where can we go?" Solomol asked the other men. "We know we can't go back to the south."

"First, is my father all right?" Malik asked Tuhuy. "Please take me to him."

"Follow me," Tuhuy replied, leading his nephew away from the crows. "I have doctored him, and he will be fine."

Meanwhile, the others continued to discuss their next move.

"Some of our Yokuts people already relocated across the mountains to the east," Limik said. "We could possibly join them."

"Runners told us that disease and drought have already taken their toll on food sources there," Tukuyun answered.

Tuhuy and Malik reached the house where Kilik and Kai-ina were living. Malik rushed to his father's side. The man had a paste made of medicinal herbs spread across one shoulder and the side of one leg.

"Father, are you all right?" the worried young man asked.

"Well, I won't be raiding ranches any time soon," Kilik replied with a smile.

"I'm so sorry for running off to live with our enemies," Malik said. "It was a foolish thing to do. Can you ever forgive me?"

"Our past is behind us," his father answered. "Nothing can be done to change it. But you are here now, and together we can look to the future. That's what's important."

Kilik extended his good arm to his son and accepted his embrace. Then the young man broke the news he'd brought from the ranch to his parents. Kilik asked to be helped to his feet. He wanted to hear what the people of the village were discussing.

Back outside, Alapay had continued translating the Yokuts discussions into Spanish for Mariposa. The Miwok woman stepped forward to speak to the group who stood in a circle around her.

My people, the Miwok, are north of here," she said as Alapay translated. "They live between the place where two rivers meet and the blue mountain lake, and I know they will take us in."

"Who is this woman?" Kilik asked his son as they reached the circle.

"Father, this is the woman I will marry," Malik replied. "I trust her with my life."

The father and son stepped into the circle, where the young man formally introduced Mariposa to his father.

"Can she lead us to the Miwok lands?" Kilik asked after he had greeted the woman.

After translating his father's question to Mariposa and then listening to her response, Malik said, "Yes, but we must stay close to the eastern mountain range to avoid the settlements of the foreigners."

Sometimes in heated debate, tribal elders and leaders discussed the strengths and weaknesses of the various options they had. After a few minutes, Kilik spoke for the group.

"Our council of leaders and elders have decided to follow Mariposa's plan," he said. "Now we must prepare for this journey."

The people returned to their homes to once again uproot their lives in order to survive.

"And as we prepare for our escape," Kilik told Malik, "You must tell me more about your experiences while you were among the strangers and about this woman you're going to marry."

Over the next day and a half, the people of Tukuyun's village gathered their belongings and dismantled their homes while lookouts kept a watch to the west.

On the morning of the third day since Malik learned of the impending attack, about two hundred people followed Mariposa as she led them northward.

Kilik was still too injured to walk or ride, so it was his turn to ride on a sled being pulled behind his horse. This was the way the injured Malik and Tuhuy were transported away from Pacheco's ranch when Kilik and Diego rescued them. As before, a few of the Natives wore the clothes of the Mexican people and traveled near the front. Scouts moved ahead and behind the main cluster of travelers.

Since Mariposa had been away from her tribe's homelands for a while, she didn't know that big changes had come to the region. Just north of the Sierra Miwok's homeland, a Swiss immigrant named Johann (John) Sutter had obtained a large land grant from the Mexican government and built a fortified settlement at the spot Mariposa described as "the place where two rivers meet." He and several hundred other immigrants from the U.S. and other parts of the world were among the first non-Spanish speaking settlers to come to California.

But the Miwok woman successfully led the people of Tukuyun's village to a village not far from her own home village. After they arrived, she was led to the village chief Loknee, whose name meant "Rain Coming Through."

After Mariposa gave Loknee a full explanation of the situation in the Miwok language, the chief agreed to let the refugees settle nearby.

Mariposa told Tuhuy and Malik about the chief and his permission to stay. This time Tuhuy was the one who was delighted to discover a Native man from another tribe with a name whose meaning was similar to his: Rain. With Mariposa to act as translator, the Chumash healer hoped in the near future to discuss medicinal treatments and tribal traditions with Loknee.

On horseback, the cousins Malik and Alapay, along with other warriors, made quick work of exploring the area to become familiar with the landscape. Experience had taught them to locate vantage points from which they could watch for strangers and defend themselves from attack.

Through Mariposa, the new arrivals began to learn about the flora and fauna of the region—what was edible, what was medicinal, what plants could be used for baskets and other utensils, and where wild game was still available.

Kilik, of course, was still healing. Kai-ina got him settled in a new shelter and Tuhuy continued to treat his shoulder and leg wounds. At age fifty-six, the experienced fighter had to accept the fact he could no longer shoot a bow and arrow, steal horses for food, or fight the enemies of his people. The muscles, ligaments and bones of his wounded shoulder were too damaged for that.

But he remembered an Indian man he met while living in Diego's camp. This man used a unique weapon Kilik had never seen before, a weapon common to the Indians of Central America. The weapon, called a sling, was made of two lengths of braided cord attached in the middle with a small pouch.

A projectile, such as a stone, was placed in the pouch. Then the warrior would hold the two ends of the cord together in one hand and swing the sling in an arc overhead. Releasing one end of the sling at the right moment caused the projectile to be thrown at a very fast speed. With practice, the slinger could injure an enemy or take down a small animal.

Kilik successfully assembled a sling and began practicing with it. As ammunition, he used the musket balls he'd kept from Tonto's Mexican wagon train. Within a few days, he was able to hit whatever target he aimed at.

Tuhuy found that the Miwok lifestyle included many similarities to the Chumash traditional ways, but there were some differences in the plants and animals in that area.

His daughter, Alapay, began to reconnect with nature. She could once again feel spiritual energy flowing from the natural world into her own being. It felt good to be back in her rightful place, and she quickly begin to learn some of the Miwok language.

The family felt at home among the Miwok people and believed they could have a peaceful life there. Within a matter of weeks, Malik and Mariposa were married in the Chumash way, and life began anew for the people who once lived at the Place of River Turtles.

But outside the world known to California's Indians, a rapid series of events began taking place that would forever impact their lives, decrease their chances of survival and lead to their almost total destruction.

In January of 1848, one of John Sutter's employees, James Marshall, discovered a nugget of a yellow, shiny metal in the South Fork of the American River near where he was building a water-driven mill. Testing proved that it was gold. Sutter wanted to keep the discovery a secret, but word got out anyway.

That same year, which was two years after that U.S. ship anchored in Monterey Bay, Mexico was defeated in the Mexican-American War. Alta California soon became a U.S. territory, opening up the area for more American settlers.

By 1849, news of the gold discovery had spread across the entire world, creating a massive migration of gold seekers who came to the region expecting to strike it rich. Tens of thousands of "forty-niners" arrived that year seeking their fortune. Boom towns and cities quickly sprang up in northern California filled with merchants ready to feed, clothe and equip those who'd been bitten with gold fever.

That same year, the California state's first constitution was signed in Monterey, and the state was officially founded in September of 1850. The newly elected members of state government began passing laws to govern the people there. None of those laws were friendly to the area's original inhabitants.

By the end of that year, much of the easily accessible gold had been found, mined and cashed in. A continual flow of gold-crazed miners from the U.S. and overseas pushed the search for more ore across the plains, river valleys and mountains of northern California. Of course, thousands of Native American people, belonging to different tribes and speaking many different languages, already lived in those areas.

Very aware of the booming population and the rush for gold, the state legislature passed a law that made it legal for white settlers to kidnap, sell or enslave Native American men, women and children even though the law was carefully worded so as not to use any terms related to slavery. The clever wording of the law, known as An Act for the Government and Protection of Indians, concealed its true intent.

Chapter 10 – A War of Extermination

Not all of the Americans who came to California in those days, however, were ready to participate in the forced labor or mass murder of indigenous peoples. One such man was Henry Jamieson, a newspaper reporter from Washington, D.C., who came to San Francisco to work for the newly established *Daily Alta California* newspaper.

In his early days as a reporter, Henry had been assigned to cover the American Indians who traveled from their homeland to the United States capital to sign treaties or ask for the government's help.

He became fascinated with these indigenous people who had lived on their lands for generations without ruining it. What the young man witnessed over and over again, however, was the U.S. government's failure to keep its promises to the Indians.

That prompted him to travel to several Indian reservations in eastern states to investigate living conditions in those communities. To prepare for the trip, the young man purchased both short and long barrel weapons and learned how to use them. His boss at the newspaper paid for the guns because he didn't want Henry traveling to "uncivilized" territories without a means of protecting himself.

What he found on those reservation was starvation and disease, because the U.S. government had broken its treaty promises to the tribes. Those people had given up their lands in exchange for food, medicine and education. Henry's truthful portrayals weren't all that popular among readers in Washington, D.C.

When the reporter heard about the gold rush and the thousands of people who were headed for California, he wanted to see it for himself. As a newspaper man, he knew there would be a wealth of news to report and stories to write.

And he wanted to see if the leaders of the new territory would behave any better towards its first inhabitants, the Indians, than the rest of the nation had.

He thought he'd probably be the only person trying to provide a fair and even view of what was going on in the gold fields, which were located in the homelands of indigenous people. He also thought his point of view might be unpopular with most of the readers of the new newspaper, who were the very people claiming Indian lands for themselves.

After arriving in San Francisco, he spent the first few days at the *Daily Alta California* reading earlier copies of the paper. He found pretty much exactly what he expected to find, that most of their news articles about raids on Indian villages praised the killing of Indians. The raids were being carried out by miners and groups of citizens who acted on rumors, not facts.

Henry then met with the newspaper's editor, Edward Dodge, and proposed that he be allowed to travel to the gold fields and observe first-hand what was going on.

"Are you sure you want to do that?" the newspaper editor asked. "You look like a city boy with little experience traveling in the back woods and camping out in the middle of nowhere surrounded by wild Indians."

"That's where you're wrong, Mr. Dodge," Henry replied. "I traveled and lived among the Indians in three states back east to observe and write about their lives and living conditions. This should be a similar experience."

"This is a very different experience, I assure you," the editor said. "According to the reports of militia commanders and miners, these Indians will sneak up on you, kill you in your sleep and then rob you blind."

Henry had heard these prejudiced words and views in his last job and wasn't interested in hearing them again. He turned to leave the editor's office, but before opening the door he said with a smile, "I promise if that happens to me, I won't blame you, Mr. Dodge."

The reporter opened the door and started to leave.

"All right!" the editor said angrily. "I see you're determined to do this whether I agree or not. Make sure you get receipts for all your expenses and turn them in. I expect to see amazing news stories from the gold fields to justify this extra expense!"

"Sure thing," Henry said as he walked out the door whistling a tune.

Within a couple of days, the reporter had gathered the gear he'd need for his journey and purchased two horses with saddles and saddlebags.

The best horse of the two he would ride. The other would serve as his pack animal. The only weapons he brought with him were his pen and paper, weapons he hoped to use in the fight against ignorance and prejudice.

Map in hand, Henry rode northeast from San Francisco toward Sutter's Mill, the place where the gold rush began, on the south fork of the American River. In no hurry, he took his time to become familiar with the terrain and his two horses, which he named Lewis and Clark.

As he began his life in the backwoods of northern California, the "civilized" folks in Sacramento continued their campaign to officially eliminate the state's Indians, along with their sources of food and the places they'd lived for centuries.

In 1851, the state's first elected governor, Peter Burnett, declared that "a war of extermination will continue to be waged between the races, until the Indian race becomes extinct." And the following year, the state legislature authorized the expenditure of over one million dollars to pay for "expeditions against the Indians."

The ultimate result of these political changes was the creation of blood-thirsty, armed militias who set out to rid the region of its "Indian problem" through the most violent means while getting paid by the state for their actions.

Henry traveled throughout northern California documenting the ever-widening search for gold and the raids conducted to eliminate any Natives who happened to live near gold deposits. In 1852, one such raid was carried out about two hundred miles north of San Francisco after a few Wintu Indians stole several head of cattle.

The local sheriff organized a volunteer squad of about forty men to punish any Indians they found. According to Henry's newspaper story, "Every man was required to swear that no living thing bearing Indian blood should escape them."

The reporter rode along with the killing party, writing down details of their escapades. Once the white men had finished their sordid task, they returned home proudly carrying more than one hundred human scalps. These had been collected from heads of the Native villagers who had been slaughtered at sunrise.

In his newspaper story, Henry was careful to mention that the punishment for white men who stole horses or cattle was jail time. But for Indians, the punishment was death. And in reality, any Indians found after the crime was committed were targeted, guilty or not.

After a couple of years, the editor of the *Daily Alta California* told Henry that soon the newspaper would no longer print stories about how bad the Indians were being treated.

"Most of our readers want to know that the state's economy is booming because of gold," Mr. Dodge said. "They want to see stories about the brave men and women pioneers who are creating a new civilized society out of the wilderness. They want to read about the new laws and policies their courageous legislators are passing to free us of those pesky Indians. That's what sells newspapers."

Of course, no California Indians were informed of these new laws and policies. However, from her home in Monterey, Magdalena followed news of these changes with a growing sense of horror as they began to appear in the pages of a growing crop of new California newspapers. She wanted desperately to find Andrea and warn her family of the impending dangers that might soon impact them. But the Mexican woman had no way of finding her friend.

Alapay's family first became aware that something had changed when she and Malik were following a deer trail they'd used many times while hunting in the area. The path ran westward along a river known to the Miwok people as the Kosumme or Salmon River.

Kilik had recovered from his wounds but was no shape to travel on long hunting trips. And because of his age, his eyes weren't as keen as they'd once been. His response time was now slower than before. These limitations further frustrated the experienced warrior, hunter and outlaw, but he knew it was time to let the next generation take over more responsibilities.

So, Malik, who was in the lead on this particular day, rounded a turn in the path and froze completely still. He motioned for Alapay to do the same. They both ducked behind a large boulder that was twice their height, which sat beside the path.

Climbing up and peeking over the boulder, Kilik's son saw three men with pale colored skin kneeling on the bank of the river. Two small horses munched grass at the river's edge, each loaded with saddle bags, guns and camping gear.

Each man held a flat metal pan containing water and some river silt mixed with tiny pebbles. The men laughed and talked to one another as they sloshed the silt around in the pans. They seemed to be looking for something within that silt.

The Natives strained to hear what the men were saying, but Malik could not make out any understandable words. Alapay, on the other hand, recognized their language.

"Those men are speaking the language called English," she told her companions in a whisper. "The same language Mr. Larkin used at times in Monterey. Thanks to my friend Magdalena, I learned to understand a little of their talk."

Malik climbed down from the top of the boulder and helped his cousin take his place so she could have a better vantage point from which to listen. After hearing them talk for a few minutes, Alapay motioned to her cousin to help her down.

"One of the men was saying they must be the first white men to come this far up river," Alapay reported in a whisper. "Another one said he thought it would be safe to camp here over night while they searched. The third man said he hoped there were no Indians around because the woods were crawling with them."

"This is a little strange," Malik commented. "What do you think they're searching for?"

Before Alapay could answer, gunfire rang out on the other side of the boulder, followed by angry shouting. The three men in the river headed for the weapons they'd placed within easy reach on their saddles.

Malik jumped back up to the top of the boulder so he could see what was happening. He saw five more pale-skinned men running up the river trail with guns in hand. Gunfire continued as the two groups shot at each other. One of the men panning for gold got hit with a bullet. He screamed in pain and fell into the water.

The other two miners grabbed him and began dragging him toward the boulder that Malik and Alapay were hiding behind.

"Run for it," Malik said in a loud whisper. "Let them shoot it out."

The two Natives ran off in different zig-zag paths deeper into the woods and away from the river. When they were a safe distance away, they met up again.

"We've got to get back to the village and warn everyone that a new and different kind of stranger has come into their homelands," Malik said, a little out of breath.

"Maybe other Native villages have seen these men as well," Alapay added. "We should send out runners to find out what neighboring tribes have seen."

As they talked, the gunfire ended.

"Maybe they've killed each other," Alapay said hopefully.

Chapter 11 – Death at Dawn

Back in the Miwok village, the cousins described to Loknee and the others what they'd seen.

"Runners have also recently brought disturbing news from our coastal Miwok brothers," Loknee admitted. "Armed groups of these white strangers have begun attacking them for no reason."

A murmur of chatter spread among the gathered people as they discussed this news.

"But I never thought their troubles would visit us here," he continued. "These hostile newcomers seem to have made our destruction their goal."

This caused louder chatter to rise among the people.

Speaking in Samala Chumash, Malik spoke to his father, telling him that they need to send out riders to other villages. Kilik agreed, so Malik asked Mariposa to translate his words to her people.

"We need to send out riders to nearby tribes to find out if the white strangers have brought trouble to them," he said. "My cousin and I are fast travelers by horse and should be able to make a round trip within a few days."

Loknee consulted others in his Elders Council, and Malik could tell they agreed with the plan by the nodding of their ancient heads.

"We would be forever in your debt if you will make these dangerous journeys on our behalf," Loknee said, speaking for the council. "We will send you with provisions."

Malik had been trying to find just the right time to give his family some news, but that opportunity never seemed to present itself. He thought now would be as good a time as any.

"Before we go, I have an announcement," he said in a loud voice, pulling Mariposa close to him and waiting for everyone's attention. "We are going to have a baby."

With broad smiles on their faces, the proud grandparents-to-be hugged the couple. This would be Kilik and Kai-ina's first grandchild. The other family members also crowded in to congratulate the expectant mother and father.

Malik kissed his wife, and then joined Alapay in preparing for their scouting trip. They gathered up the dried foods Loknee provided, and headed through the woods and away from the village. Using the position of Grandfather Sun in the sky and natural landmarks described by the chief, they headed for neighboring villages made up of the Nisenan Indian people who were part of the Maidu tribes.

A full day's ride took them to the fork of the American River they were searching for. According to Chief Loknee, a string of villages lay alongside the river as it came down from the mountains to the east.

Looking upriver, Alapay saw a pillar of smoke rising above the tree line.

"That must be smoke from a cooking fire in the first village," she said. "We don't want to startle the people there, so let's dismount and walk in."

Tying their horses to nearby trees, the two scouts hiked the short distance to the village carrying their bows and arrows. What they found was a sight so horrifying it caused Alapay to cry out and Malik to drop to the ground on his knees.

Before them lay the burnt-out homes of the village. Scattered around those smoking hulls were bodies of the men, women and children who once lived in those homes. They had been attacked. Some had fallen as they apparently attempted to flee.

"Who would do such a thing?" Alapay asked as she walked closer to the ghastly scene.

Malik didn't answer. He couldn't answer. He couldn't even speak. Finally, he stood up and moved in beside his cousin.

"This reminds me of the time the Place of Condors was raided by the men of *ranchero* Francisco Pacheco," Malik said. "But most of us were kidnapped, not killed. Remember?"

"I do," Alapay answered. "But this is a lot worse than that."

The pair slowly walked through the site trying to learn what had happened.

"This must've been a surprise attack," Malik said as he stood over the body of one man. "You see that none of the men died with weapons in their hands. They didn't have time to get them."

Alapay, who had inherited some of her father's spiritual gifts, walked over to the deceased body of a Nisenan woman. She knelt down and place one hand on the woman's forehead. Closing her eyes and saying a brief prayer, Alapay then called on a spirit helper to reveal what had happened here. In a few moments more, she felt a vibrational energy course through her body. Images began to appear in her mind, showing her the village at dawn.

The Nisenan people were asleep in their homes. Then there was movement in the woods around the village. White men with long guns and pistols stepped from behind trees and began firing into the homes.

People screamed as they awoke and tried to flee. The men with guns moved in closer and began shooting as Natives came out of their houses. Other men with long knives charged toward the settlement, too.

Alapay opened her eyes and shook her head to clear the terrible vision away.

After taking a moment to recover from those sights and sounds she said, "The attackers were the white strangers, like the ones we saw near our village the other day."

"They've come in search of something," Malik said. "Something they value more than human life."

After standing quietly in the village for a few more moments, Alapay said, "We have a job to do so we need to get on with it. We have to find out if this has happened in other places and report back."

Without another word, the two walked back to their horses.

Before riding on toward the next village site, Malik advised, "We must move cautiously from now on. We may run into the men who did this to our brothers. They seem to travel in well-armed groups."

Malik and Alapay understood that their scouting trip had become a dangerous one that required total alertness at all times.

Just then they heard the sound of hoof beats coming up the trail toward them. Pulling out his bow, Malik nocked an arrow and readied himself for an attack. Seeing a tree with low hanging branches next to the trail, Alapay climbed up on one of the branches and waited.

Malik stepped behind a tree so he could surprise whoever was coming toward them.

Soon a single white man came riding into view, leading a pack horse behind him. After the stranger passed under her, Alapay leapt from the branch. She landed on the horse's back right behind the man. As she did so, Malik stepped from behind the tree and aimed an arrow at the man's chest. Then Alapay grabbed the man's arms from behind, preventing him from moving.

"Please don't shoot," the man yelled in fear. "I'm unarmed and I'm not here to hurt you."

Malik, not understanding the man's words, kept his arrow aimed at his chest.

Alapay, who understood his words, relaxed the pressure on his arms. Also, since she could easily sense his intensions and character, she felt he was no threat.

"Relax," she told Malik in Chumash. "I can talk his talk."

As her cousin eased up on the bow, she jumped down from the horse and walked around to the front of the animal.

"Get down," she told the man who looked a little different from the other white men she'd seen. Those men had scruffy beards and untidy hair.

This man was well-groomed. The others wore dirty, smelly clothes and didn't seem to bathe. This man smelled a little like elderberry blossoms, and his clothes seemed to be of better quality.

"Where did you come from and why are you here?" Alapay asked in English as he dismounted.

"My name is Henry Jamieson, and I assure you I mean no harm," he replied.

"You didn't answer my question," Alapay said.

"Oh, right," Henry said. "I came from San Francisco. I am a newspaper reporter and I'm here to write stories about how gold mining is effecting you Indians."

"What's he saying?" Malik asked impatiently in Samala. "What's he saying?"

"Wait!" Alapay replied sharply, also in Samala. "Don't rush me!"

"You came from San Francisco," Alapay said to Henry. "How did you come from Saint Francis? I do not understand."

"You must live in a very remote area if you don't know that San Francisco is the name of a city," he answered. "How is it that you know English?"

"I am asking the questions!" she replied angrily. "What is gold mining?"

Henry stuck his hand in the front pocket of his pants and pulled something out. He held it up for the cousins to see. It was a small gold nugget. Malik eased up on his bow and put his arrow back in the quiver.

He took the nugget from Henry to examine it more closely. Then he handed it to Alapay.

"That, my friends, is gold," Henry said. "That's what thousands of people have come to California to find. Gold mining is what they're doing to find it and dig it out of the ground."

Alapay handed the nugget back and then translated the entire conversation to Malik.

"Show me this gold mining," she told Henry.

"I can take you to a nearby gold mining operation," Henry said, "If you will allow me to live with you and your tribe for a while. I am recording what these white men are doing in your Native lands."

"We will follow you to the gold mining, but we have to speak to our village elders about you living with us," Alapay replied.

"All right," the reporter said. "First things first."

Alapay said something to Malik in their tongue before speaking to Henry again.

"If you want to see what the white men are doing when they are not digging for gold, we will show you," she said. "Follow us."

All three of them mounted their horses. Malik led the way back to the burnt-out village.
Henry was as shocked and horrified as the two Natives had been. He dismounted and walked through the scene. Afterwards, he returned to his horse, removing a pen and notebook from one of the saddlebags. He began describing the scene on paper.

When he'd finished he said, "I have witnessed similar scenes in other places, and I must ride to my office to turn in this report."

He got on his horse and said, "The gold mining site is on my way so I'll take you there first."

Chapter 12 – Follow Orders

They traveled downhill for a while following the stream.
Then they turned north and rode until they came to another
stream just as the sun was setting.

"We should camp here for the night," Henry said.
"The mining operation is just a little further down this
stream."

That night, before going to sleep, Alapay and Malik
talked about the white stranger named Henry.

"I don't think we should trust him," Malik said. "He
could be lying to us about who he is and what he's doing out
here."

"I feel nothing but honesty from him," Alapay
replied. "And I think he's kind of cute."

"What!?" Malik sat straight up. "That's crazy."

"It's obvious he's very smart," she continued. "I think he really wants to help our people."

"Never mind," Malik said, lying back down. "Forget I said anything about him."

Alapay fell asleep thinking of the way Henry smelled. Elderberry blossoms.

At sunrise the following morning, Malik awoke to a strange sound coming from further downriver. He'd never heard anything like it before. Quickly he woke his cousin, gesturing for her to keep quiet and listen. She, too, heard this repetitive "chugging" noise from down the river.

Henry was already awake and saddling his horse.

"After I show you the mining operation, I have to ride to San Francisco to get the story of the latest massacre printed," Henry said. "That's my job."

He approached Alapay.

"But after that, I do want to live among your people," he told her, reaching out to take her hand. "I especially want to come back to you, Alapay, because, well—"

Alapay blushed.

Malik said, "I think I'm going to be sick."

"Close your mouth, cousin," Alapay said as she gazed into Henry's eyes. "I am busy with girl stuff right now."

Malik said, "I know I'm going to be sick."

Henry and Alapay, two people from two entirely different worlds, continued gazing into one another's eyes.

"We'd better get a move on!" Malik said loudly in Spanish this time. "We have a job to do. He has a job to do. We should get busy doing those jobs."

That broke the spell the two were under. Each of them looked around and realized the reality of what Malik had said. They also realized all of them could understand and speak Spanish so they now had a way for all three of them could communicate.

"Vamonos," Henry said.

Leaving their horses behind, they crept quietly down river and toward the sound. Using boulders, bushes and trees for cover, they made their way to the source of the noise. Peering over the top of a large fallen tree, they beheld an unfamiliar sight.

A device near the water was making the chugging sound. It belched dark smoke into the air as a wheel on its side turned 'round and round. More than a dozen people worked nearby digging holes, hauling mud and dumping it into wooden troughs. Water surged through the troughs washing away the mud but leaving behind pebbles and shiny pieces of the flaked yellow stone.

Surprisingly, a few of the workers were Natives. They seemed to be doing the hardest work, watched over by the white strangers. One of the white watchers carried a whip that he used on a Native if he or she didn't work fast enough.

Then, one white stranger who studied the water-filled trough, plunged a hand in the water and excitedly yelled "Eureka" very loudly. When he pulled his hand out of the water, it contained a lump of gold, which he held up for all to see.

All the workers stopped to look at the object the man held. One of the white watchers cracked his whip, yelling at the Native workers. They returned to their back-breaking chores.

Malik had seen enough and signaled for the three of them to slip away and move back up stream. Once they reached the spot they'd left their horses, he began to speak.

"So that's gold mining," he said. "They don't realize how much they are harming the rivers, fish and other wildlife with their search for gold. But I don't know why they value it so highly."

"It is clear that these new foreigners treat Indians the same way other foreigners have," Alapay said. "Either they enslave us or kill us, which ever suits their needs."

"Now that you've seen why these men have come into your lands, you need to warn your people," Henry said. "Gold miners will stop at nothing to get what they're after."

Malik said, "I agree with our new friend."

Alapay was surprised and pleased to hear her cousin call Henry a friend.

"Yes, and I hope my father can seek guidance from the spirits of our ancestors to find out what we should do now," Alapay replied. "He has always been able to lead us in that way."

All three of them left that territory with heavy hearts. The two Natives had witnessed death and destruction never before imaginable—the senseless death of their brothers and sisters and the destruction of the natural landscapes of Mother Earth.

Henry's words echoed in Alapay's mind. She feared that the intentions and actions of these new strangers would lead to the ultimate destruction of their ancient way of Native life. The death of their relationship to the land. The eventual death of all Native people.

Before Henry headed off towards San Francisco, he asked Alapay, "How will I find you again when I return?"

"We must set a meeting place," she said. "How many days from now will you come back?"

"Five or six days, I think," the reporter said.

"Meet me where the Kosumme River meets the Mokelumne River in six days," she said. "Can you find that?"

"I will find it one way or another," Henry answered. "See you then."

After climbing on his horse, he gave Alapay one last look and rode west.

With extra vigilance, the two cousins rode back toward their village, this time taking a different route so they could visit one more Nisenan location on the way. Evening overtook the scouts before they reached that village so they rested for the night in a shallow cave they found.

Earlier in the day, Malik had managed to spear a salmon that swam in a stream they crossed. Now, using the traditional fire-starter kit they'd brought, which consisted of a round stone, a piece of flint and a wad of kindling, the young man lit a fire at the mouth of the shelter. The fresh fish tasted particularly good after the dried foods they'd been eating the last few days.

Light from their small cooking fire danced on the stone walls of the little cavern. Alapay noticed faded red and black images on those walls. She picked up a branch and stuck its tip into the flames. When the branch ignited, she carried it with her for better lighting so she could examine the images more closely.

"The Native people here must have marked these walls with spirit images in much the same way our Chumash people did back home," she said. "Once, my father drew some of the images for me and explained their purpose. He said they were prayer paintings used to ask spirit beings for their help."

"I am certain that you and Uncle Tuhuy know more about such matters than I ever will," Malik replied.

They sat in silence gazing into the fire for a while. A tiredness of both body and mind settled into them as the flames died down, and they prepared for sleep. But Alapay had one more thing to add before they closed their eyes for the night.

"I've never set foot in the lands of our ancestors," she said. "One day I hope to. I wander what it was like."

There was no response. Snoring was the only sound to be heard.

Alapay and Malik awoke at sunrise the following morning. The young man was in a mischievous mood and began kidding his cousin about her attraction to Henry.

"I'm looking forward to watching you explain to your Father why he should accept this white man into our lives," he said. "There's no way he'll agree."

"Don't be so sure, cousin," Alapay replied. "I convinced him to let me live among the strangers in Monterey, didn't I?"

The two continued their back-and-forth banter as they rode away from their overnight camping place. But soon they became focused on the day's journey, their final village visit. Malik really dreaded it, too. Would they witness more death and destruction? He hoped not.

Riding southward from the foothills to a lower elevation, the duo had a wide view of the valley below. Stretched out before them in the distance is what looked like a line of soldiers on horseback. In front of the soldiers was a cluster of people on foot.

Malik wanted a closer look but didn't want to alert the soldiers to their presence. He suggested that Alapay stay put while he moved in closer.

"Absolutely not," the young woman said. "We stick together."

Her cousin shrugged his shoulders and began having his horse thread its way through the underbrush to get a better view. Alapay followed. Soon they had moved close enough to leave their horses behind and travel on foot.

Staying behind a line of trees that grew along a creek, the two were able to come close enough to study the soldiers' uniforms and hear what they were saying. Their outfits were made of dark blue cloth highlighted by a row of bright brass buttons. On their heads they wore dark blue wide-brimmed hats.

The lead rider carried a small red and white triangular flag. They were white men and not Mexicans. Each had a pistol in a holster on his hip. Some also brandished swords.

In front of the soldiers marched a line of very thin and tired-looking Indians who carried baskets and cloth bags. Men, women and children shuffled along, goaded by the soldiers who laughed if one of the Natives stumbled or fell to the ground.

Malik stiffened in anger at the sound of their laughter. He started to pull his bow from behind his back, but his cousin stopped him.

"We are outnumbered," she whispered. "Now be quiet so I can listen to what they're saying."

Malik put the bow back in its place and just glared at Alapay.

"It'd save ever body a lot of time and trouble if we just killed these God-forsaken Injuns instead of marching 'em off to some stockade," one soldier said to another.

"Shut your trap and follow orders," the other one replied. "These people would get murdered in their sleep if they stayed in their own village."

"That might be more humane," the first one said. "They'll probably starve to death at the stockade like the last batch we delivered there."

"Cut the chit chat, men!" their commander ordered. "Keep your eyes open for vigilantes and local militia. You know they're out to kill every last Injun in this state!"

Alapay whispered to Malik, "They speak English so they must be American soldiers."

The two cousins remained still and quiet until the procession moved away. Then they made it back to their horses.

"Time to get back home and tell our people what we've seen," Malik said. "It will be hard for them to believe that these things are even possible. It's hard for me to believe!"

Back in their village, Malik and Alapay met with their tribal leaders and described the three scenes they'd witnessed.

"These are terrible times we live in," Tuhuy said after hearing the cousins' report.

"Are we to believe these things actually happened?" Tukuyun asked angrily. "The things you say are unbelievable!"

It sounded to Alapay like the chief thought she and Malik were lying.

"We wouldn't believe them either," Alapay replied defensively, "If we hadn't seen them with our own eyes."

"Daughter, you and Malik should go and get some food while I talk with Tukuyun and the others about these events," Alapay's father suggested. "We need to have some serious discussions now."

The cousins were tired and hungry so they gladly left their elders to talk, and possibly argue, among themselves.

Chapter 13 – Pay Good Money

In San Francisco, Henry turned in his news story about the massacre of Nisenan people he'd witnessed with Malik and Alapay. After reading it, Mr. Dodge, the newspaper editor, wadded up the paper the story was written on and threw it in a trash can.

"Why did you do that?" Henry asked, shocked at his editor's action.

"Because I won't be printing it," he replied. "As I told you before, our readers aren't interested in these kinds of stories. This is 1855, and my newspaper now has a new editorial policy. We will only be printing stories that support the actions of our state government and the rights of the state's three-hundred-thousand new American residents."

"What about fair and balanced reporting?" Henry asked angrily. "Are you abandoning the first rule of newspaper publishing?"

"The first rule of newspaper publishing is to keep the presses running, to keep the business going," Mr. Dodge said, getting up from behind his desk. "So, I will no longer be needing your services, Mr. Jamieson. It's time for you to empty out your desk, pick up your final paycheck and move on."

Henry was angry, sad and disappointed all at the same time. He wanted to punch Dodge in the mouth but didn't. Then an idea came to him.

"Thank you, Mr. Dodge," he said with a smile. "You've just made it possible for me to start writing the book I've always wanted to write."

He turned and headed for the door.

"It's all about my experiences living with the Indians," he said before leaving. "There's a book publisher I know back in Washington who'll print it and distribute it all over the country!"

Slamming the editor's door behind him, Henry began to think about the fascinating Native woman he was going to meet in two days. She was beautiful, smart, athletic and mysterious—like no other woman he'd ever met.

He certainly hoped her father was going to allow him to live with her people.

The following morning, back in their village in Miwok territory, Tuhuy called for a family meeting like the one they had before leaving the Hidden Place all those years ago. Solomol, who was now seventy-nine years old, had fallen ill during the night and was resting. They held the meeting at his house where Tuhuy's mother, Yol, was caring for him. Kilik and Kai-ina, Tuhuy and Taya, Malik and Mariposa, and, of course, Alapa all gathered.

"I've called us all together so we can talk about what's been happening in our lives and what we may need to do in the future," Tuhuy said. "This area is becoming more dangerous for us than anywhere we've lived before. What we're going to do about that?"

"What are our choices?" Solomol asked between coughs.

"We can stay here with our extended families and friends," Kilik said. "That would probably mean we'd be fighting for our lives alongside them."

"We could search for a new place to move to," Malik offered. "But tribes further north are being wiped out by the white strangers."

"Our elders, Solomol and Yol, have told me they'd like to once again see the Place of River Turtles," Tuhuy said. "But I'm not sure how we'd survive the long trip back south. The lands between here and our home are filled with strangers who still want to capture or kill us."

"Father, have you used the Eyes of the Condor ceremony to see what is happening back at the Place of River Turtles?" Alapay asked.

"I have tried, but something is interfering with my ability to see with spiritual eyes," Tuhuy answered. "I'm not sure what the problem is."

"Maybe we should each think about our choices and come back together in a couple of days," Kilik recommended. "Our dream helpers might provide us with some answers during the night."

As the family dispersed, Alapay asked to speak to her father and mother alone. When the rest of the family members had left, she began telling them her story.

"I met a man who I've invited to come and live with us," she said.

"That's good, my child," Tuhuy said. "We all need a companion in our lives. What tribe is he from?"

"He's not from any tribe," she answered. "He's a white man. His name is Henry."

Alapay's mother and father said nothing. They were too shocked to think of anything to say.

"He has a good heart and has been telling other white men how badly Indians have been treated," she added. "And I like him very much."

"You can't trust a white man," Tuhuy proclaimed. "They are all focused on obtaining material things—objects and land and money."

"When I lived in Monterey, the head of the house was a nice white man," Alapay replied. "Mr. Larkin was respectful, and didn't talk badly about Indians. I learned to talk English from him."

"So you told us," Taya answered, then paused a moment. "What is this Henry like?"

"He is different," she said. "He understands what we've been through since the strangers have come onto our lands. And I felt his inner being. There was truth and honesty there. I want you to meet him."

"How is he even going to find us," her mother asked. "We have lived far away from the strangers just so they can't find us."

"I am to meet him in two days where the Kosumme River meets the Mokelumne River," Alapay answered. "He said he would be able to find it."

Her parents whispered to one another for a short while, then Tuhuy spoke.

"All right, I will have this man meet Kilik, Solomol, Yol, your mother and I," he said. "After that we will discuss whether or not he can remain among us."

Alapay became very excited and thanked her parents for agreeing to meet him. She then went to tell Malik and Mariposa the news.

"You should see how she makes eyes at him," Malik told Mariposa with a chuckle. "It's enough to make you sick at your stomach."

Alapay blushed a little, saying, "Shut up, cousin. So what if I make eyes at him."

She punched him in the arm, causing him to let out a loud, "Ouch!"

"Do not make fun of her," Mariposa scolded her husband as he rubbed the spot Alapay hit. "Have you forgotten what you were like when we first met? You were all awkward and clumsy around me—a total mess!"

Now it was Malik's turn to blush.

Alapay left her cousin and his wife to prepare for her two-day ride to meet Henry.

After gathering supplies and saying goodbye, she headed out. Thoughts of the man, who was strong, tall and handsome for a white man, swirled in her head.

Approaching their meeting place in the middle of the afternoon of the second day, the Native woman saw a column of smoke rising from the corner of land where the rivers met.

That must be Henry's fire, she thought. She decided to sneak up and surprise him.

Dismounting, she quietly led her horse toward the column of smoke. As she got closer, she heard the laughter of several men coming from the camp. She froze in place. That wasn't Henry. He'd be alone.

She began to turn away when someone jumped out from behind a tree and grabbed her. It was a smelly white man with a scruffy beard. Startled, her horse ran into the nearby underbrush. She immediately began trying to fight off the husky man.

"Hey, I got one!" he yelled to the other men. "But I need help. She's a fighter!"

Before the other men reached their friend, Alapay freed one of her arms and punched her captor right in the nose.

"Ow!" he shouted. "Hurry up or she'll get away."

Three other men showed up in time to pin Alapay's arms behind her. She then started kicking at her captors, landing a blow to one fellow's knee. They all heard a crunch followed by a scream of pain as the man fell to the ground.

One of the other men slapped Alapay across the face hard leaving a welt on her cheek.

"Hold it right there!" a man's voice yelled at them from a few yards away.

Everyone looked up to see a nicely dressed white man sitting on a horse and holding some kind of pistol. The gun was aimed at the man closest to Alapay.

"Step away from the woman," Henry commanded as he pulled back the pistol's hammer.

"But, friend, we found her first," another of the men said. "There are plenty of men who would pay good money for a squaw like this one."

Henry spoke to Alapay in Spanish, pretty sure that none of these men would understand him.

"Habla solo Espaniol," he told her. "Speak only Spanish."

"What did he mean that someone would pay money for me?" she asked, also in Spanish.

"I'll tell you later," he replied, keeping his gun aimed at the man holding her. "I have an idea so go along with it for now."

Alapay nodded.

"Gentlemen, and I use the word loosely, this squaw belongs to me," the reporter said in English. "I already paid good money for her, so you can leave her and go back to searching for gold."

"Can you prove she belongs to you?" the man with the bloody nose answered. "We have her now, and there are four of us and only one of you. You may get a single shot off, but one of our four guns will take care of you."

"That's where you're wrong, mister," Henry said. "See, this gun is a brand new Colt forty-four caliber revolver, made for the U.S. Army. I can get six shots off without reloading."

"You're bluffing," one man said.

"Am I? There's one way to find out."

No one moved for a few seconds. When the man on the ground thought Henry wasn't looking, he slowly slid his pistol from its holster. A bullet from Henry's revolver hit the man before you could blink an eye. Then Henry's gun quickly returned to its original position.

"Who's next?" he asked.

The man holding Alapay released her immediately, saying, "We're very sorry for the misunderstanding. This squaw clearly belongs to you."

The three men scurried back to their camp, leaving their dead friend behind. Once he was sure the miners weren't going to return, Henry jumped down from his horse and ran to Alapay. She hugged him gratefully. He hugged her back.

"I was beginning to worry that you wouldn't show," she admitted.

"You are all I've thought about since I've been gone," he said. "I sure hope your family allows me to stay with you."

"What about your newspaper job in San Francisco?" Alapay asked.

"I don't work there anymore," he replied with a smile. "I am free to travel as I please."

She was silent for a moment.

"What was that about someone paying good money for me?" she asked.

"The state government passed a law making it legal for white men to buy and sell Indian men, women and children to use them as slave labor," Henry answered. "And they claim to be the civilized ones."

146

Alapay went quiet again, finding it hard to believe that one group of people could make up their own evil rules like that.

"We'd better find my horse and head back to the village," she said finally. "Before someone else shows up trying to sell me."

Henry got back up on his horse, and Alapay jumped up behind him. She pointed in the direction her horse had gone, and they set out in that direction. After easily finding the animal, Alapay led Henry toward her village.

Chapter 14 – Eyes of the Condor

The following day, Alapay galloped into the circle of Miwok homes with Henry and his pack horse close behind. As usual, the lookouts had already announced their arrival, so the people were already gathered to greet her.

"What happened to your cheek?" Tuhuy asked in Samala as Alapay dismounted. "Did this white man do that to you?"

"This white man's name is Henry," she answered curtly. "And he saved me from four filthy white men who captured me and wanted to sell me as a slave!"

Her father was dumbfounded by here statement. So much information was packed into that one short sentence.

Filthy white men captured his daughter and tried to sell her as a slave?

"Henry Jamieson, sir," Henry said in English, extending his hand to Tuhuy. "Happy to make your acquaintance."

"Try Spanish instead," Alapay suggested. "He speaks and understands it well."

"Perdoname," Henry said and then repeated his introduction in that language.

Not moving, Tuhuy still seemed to be trying to process his daughter's earlier statement, so Kilik stepped forward to shake Henry's hand.

Speaking in Samala, he said, "We are pleased to welcome you to our little village. My niece says you want to live with us for a while, and it sounds like you can handle yourself well."

Alapay translated her uncle's welcome.

"Spanish or English?" Henry asked of Alapay.

"Neither," she replied. "But I can translate."

Finally, seeing his cousin greeting the stranger, Tuhuy snapped out of whatever mental zone he'd been in.

"I am not used to seeing or speaking with white men," he said, also shaking Henry's hand. "I guess I'll have to get used to it."

Alapay's mother, Taya, stepped forward to introduce herself as well.

In a very gentlemanly fashion, Henry took her hand and kissed it lightly. She withdrew it suddenly, unfamiliar with that European-based gesture.

Upset, she looked to her daughter and asked, "Why did he do that?"

Alapay, in turn translated the question to Henry.

"Please excuse me again," Henry pleaded sincerely in English. "Where I come from, that is meant to communicate the utmost respect and admiration."

Alapay translated Henry's words into Samala.

Upon hearing the translation, Taya blushed a little, then smiled at Henry. She voluntarily extended her hand to the man, and Henry kissed it again. Seeing that his wife was enjoying the gesture a little too much, Tuhuy stepped up and pulled his wife away.

"Tell this man... uh, Henry, he is welcome to stay for a short while," Tuhuy said, this time deciding to speak in Samala. "We will be watching his words and actions to determine if he will be allowed to remain with us for a longer period of time."

Before leaving the group, Tuhuy called for a family meeting to be held that evening. Then he took Taya and headed for their home. Everyone else in the village quickly crowded around to get a look at Alapay's new friend and to speculate about their relationship. After a while, Alapay pulled Henry away from the crowd.

"You can stay with us for now," she told him. "Let's get you settled in."

Henry followed her with his two horses, tied them to nearby trees and placed a few of his belongings inside Alapay's bark and branch, cone-shaped house. Then he and Alapay took a hike through the nearby woods for the rest of the day.

Just before dark, everyone in Alapay's family except Solomol gathered in front of Tuhuy's home. The elder was still sick in spite of Tuhuy's regular herbal treatments.

"As we continue talking about the future of this family, we have a new source of information to include," Tuhuy said. "I'm talking about Henry."

Since Alapay's father had been speaking Samala, Henry didn't understand a word that was said until he heard his own name mentioned.

"What's he saying?" he asked Alapay in English.

"I think he wants to ask you some questions about what's going on with the strangers," she answered. "That's what we call the Mexicans and Americans that have overrun our Native lands: the strangers."

Tuhuy continued by telling Kilik that he would be talking to Henry in Spanish. Then the questioning began. Alapay was glad her father didn't offer to give Henry a bite of food for every answer he gave like they'd done with Tonto.

The whole process took about an hour, and Henry was eager to answer each question fully. Every so often Tuhuy summarized the discussion in Samala for Kilik.

Henry told them about the Mexican-American war, what happened when the Americans won that war, the discovery of gold and the following rush of newcomers, the creation of the state called California, and the laws created by the new state government. It was a lot to tell.

After all the questions had been answered and then translated, the family sat quietly by the fire for a long time. It was a lot of information to absorb, information that didn't sound good for the future of Indian people.

Finally, Tuhuy told Alapay, "I've tried three times to use the Eyes of the Condor to see the area around the Place of River Turtles, but it isn't working for me. I need you to try now."

"All right, Father," she replied. "Tomorrow I'll climb up to a higher elevation and try. Maybe from there I will have a better view."

After the family meeting broke up, Alapay told Henry she needed to start preparing for tomorrow's ceremony that night.

"I need to keep quiet and focus my energy," she said. "In the morning, I'll continue preparations by fasting and isolating myself from everyone else. You can take care of yourself, can't you?"

"Of course," he answered taking her hand. "I'll visit with your father and uncle. I think I can learn a lot from them if they'll come to trust me."

"Two of the best people I've ever known," she said. "All right, then. I'll say goodnight."

She squeezed his hand and gave him a little kiss on the cheek before heading to her house. Alone that night, Henry began jotting down notes in his journal by the light of a small fire. This was the beginning of the book he'd write about living with Native peoples.

Next morning, he joined Tuhuy, Kilik, their wives and Malik for breakfast. Henry passed the time very enjoyably as they conversed in Spanish.

Meanwhile, Alapay started getting ready for the ceremony. Using the Eyes of the Condor to see across the hundreds of miles that separated her from the Place of River Turtles required extraordinary concentration.

Her morning preparations included multiple cycles of prayers and songs. There were four sacred songs that were to be sung four times each. This was in keeping with the common Native American belief in the meaning of that number. Four directions—north, east, south, west; four seasons—winter, spring, summer, fall; four sacred colors—white, yellow, black, white; four phases of a person's life—infancy, youth, adulthood, old age.

Taking with her only a tule reed mat and a basket water bottle, Alapay then hiked up a nearby hill. A clearing at the top provided her with an ideal spot to conduct the ceremony. Spreading out her mat, she sat down cross-legged facing south towards the lands of her ancestors. Then the young medicine woman repeated the cycles of prayers and songs, while at the same time repeating her goal: seeing the homelands of the Samala Chumash People.

Her father had taught her that repetition of the words, tones and melodies altered the mind of the person who verbalized them.

The very vibrations created by those sounds moved the mind away from the physical world towards an inner world of pure energy. That's where your mind needed to be before you could jump into the condor's mind and see with his eyes. Doing that took a lot of practice.

Alapay felt herself slipping away from her physical body, moving deeper into a spiritual state of mind. Then she felt herself floating upwards into the sky above her, while her body remained on the ground. Finally, she mentally searched for a condor in flight. In a few moments, one came into mental view, and it was already flying southward, the direction she needed to go.

Almost like being propelled by an invisible sling-shot, Alapay zoomed into the bird's mind. Soon she was looking down, seeing through the condor's eyes. Feeling the power of the bird's nine-foot wingspan, the young woman sped through the air at a high altitude. Moving much faster than a condor normally could, they soon reached the valley that was the homeland of the Samala Chumash People.

Never having been there herself, she was able to recognize the area because it drew her like a magnet. Her blood was of these lands. Her father was born here. Her grandparents were born here. Unknown generations of their people had lived and died here. Her soul was home.

Alapay's father had described the spot where the Place of River Turtles had been located. She watched for a sharp curve in the river that flowed at the base of the mountain range at the edge of that valley. When she found the area she was looking for, she guided the condor closer to the ground to get a better view. It looked like the ideal site for a Chumash village, but there were no signs of tule reed homes or people living there.

Turning parallel to the river, Alapay maneuvered the bird downstream. There, along a creek that flowed into the river, were several structures made of tree trunks, branches and various lengths of wooden boards. Those could only be peoples' homes, Alapay thought, even though they didn't look like any home constructed by Native people she'd ever seen.

Hovering overhead for a short while, Alapay watched as people begin to emerge from those homes. It seemed as though they had sensed that the large, sacred bird was flying overhead. Elders, adults and children streamed out of several homes and looked up.

Again, Alapay dropped in altitude to get a better look. As she did, a collective gasp rose from the group of gathered people who felt a rush of excitement at seeing the huge bird come so close.

At the same time, Alapay felt a rush of excitement at seeing the people on the ground. They were brown-skinned Native people like herself! According to her father and her uncle, every Chumash person of their home village had long ago been rounded up and forced into the nearest mission. The land had been deserted for decades. But now, the Samala People had somehow miraculously returned to the lands of their ancestors. That was a thrilling discovery.

The excitement of seeing her people once again in their homeland jolted Alapay out of the condor's mind. With a loud swooshing sound, she found herself rapidly returning to her own human body sitting on the top of that hill hundreds of miles from the Place of River Turtles.

Chapter 15 – The Long Journey Home

Opening her eyes, she blinked several times at her bright afternoon surroundings. Thinking back over the experience she'd just had, Alapay got excited all over again.

"I did it!" she shouted as she jumped up from the mat. "I've got to go tell the family what I saw!"

Alapay's family, including Henry, anxiously gathered at Solomol's house when she came down from the hill. First, she spoke in Samala, and then self-translated to English. Everyone, especially Henry, was amazed at the experiences she described and the sights she saw.

"Does that mean we could actually go home?" Solomol asked, sicker and weaker than ever.

"Oh, I hope so," Yol said. "That would mean a lot to both Solomol and me."

"We'd have to scout out the route very carefully," Kilik said. "The land between here and there is treacherous, filled with dangerous strangers."

"Kilik is right," Tuhuy said. "We have to do something more than wear our old, worn out Mexican clothing as disguises."

After hearing that conversation translated, an idea hit Henry like a thunderbolt. Speaking in English, he said, "I have an idea that might work."

"Switch to Spanish so my father and cousin can understand too," Alapay said.

"It's a terrible thing, but the law of the land says that a white man can own Indians as laborers," Henry said in Spanish.

Malik translated this to Samala for his father.

"During the trip south, we could pretend that I own all of you," he continued. "If anyone stops us or tries to interfere with our journey, I'll claim that you are my property."

Malik translated.

"We are no man's property!" Kilik angrily replied in Samala, jumping to his feet.

"Of course, Father," Malik responded quickly. "*Timolokich*. It's just a story."

The family spontaneously burst into a Samala debate. To Henry it seemed that Tuhuy and his cousin had very different reactions to the idea. The American let them sort through it on their own. Soon, they reached a resolution.

"We will only be using this story when we come into contact with Mexicans or Americans, correct?" Tuhuy said in Spanish.

"Then and only then," Henry agreed. "It's just a story to help us travel in peace."

Tuhuy repeated Henry's answer in Samala, to which Kilik nodded.

"*Que Bueno!*" Malik said loudly as he shook the white man's hand. "That's good!"

They decided to allow themselves a couple of days to prepare for the long journey. They gathered provisions and said their goodbyes to the Miwoks. The Miwoks, in turn, decided to hold a farewell feast for their departing friends.

During the festivities, Tuhuy had a private conversation with his mother and cousin.

"Solomol's condition is getting worse in spite of my treatments," he told them. "We need to make this three-hundred-fifty-mile trip as quickly as possible. He wants to see our homeland before he dies."

"I'll build a sled to carry him like the one we made for Tuhuy and Malik when we left Pacheco's ranch," Kilik offered. "That way he can save his energy, and we can move faster."

And so, three days after making their decision, the family set off on their perilous trip. Henry would be traveling with eight Natives, and to help "sell" their story, he would ride on horseback in the rear of the group.

Directly in front of him would be Yol on horseback towing the sled that carried Solomol. In front of the elders, Kilik, Malik and Alapay would travel on foot leading their horses. The rest of the family would travel on foot in front of the others. With his revolver in hand, this arrangement would give the appearance that Henry was keeping an eye on "his Indians."

The only real roads in California before the 1850s were short ones that connected a town to the nearest seaport, or connected two nearby towns. Otherwise there were really only trails. Some of those were wide enough in places for wagons to use.

One of the oldest trails in the region was an inland passageway that later came to be known as Stockton-Los Angeles Road. In the 1850s, this route was quickly enhanced because more gold had been discovered on the western slopes of the Sierra Nevada Mountains.

It was Henry's goal to get to that dirt road as soon as possible, because that route was the fastest way to travel south. He had learned of it while working for the *Daily Alta California* newspaper. Because it ran through areas where gold had been recently discovered, Henry was worried that unsuccessful miners might try to steal Alapay's family of Indians from him.

Fortunately, Henry had saved some of his newspaper salary in the form of gold and silver U.S. dollars. Alapay and Malik had also held on to many of the pesos they'd earned from their jobs in the Monterey area. That meant they had money to buy food and supplies for the journey, if needed.

The unusual caravan first made its way through open countryside headed to Stockton, a small town founded in 1849. During this first leg of the journey they did indeed pass groups of miners, on foot and on horseback, going to the southern gold mines. Henry could tell that some of the men eyed their group suspiciously.

Henry could almost see their minds calculating their odds of stealing the Indians away from the white man in the back of the group. In those cases, Henry merely showed them his revolver, and they quickly changed their minds.

In Stockton, Henry found the starting point for wagon trail that would provide them with a flatter and smoother surface to ride and walk on. They passed through French Camp where fur traders from the north frequently gathered. Their route continued southward and a few miles east of the San Joaquin River. At several points, ferries carried the travelers across rapidly flowing rivers.

Traveling through the San Joaquin Valley, the wagon trail took them through a small community that later became Fresno where Henry was able to buy a wagon. Malik hitched one of their horses to the wagon so the ailing Solomol would have a more comfortable ride.

Both Tuhuy and Alapay were caring for Solomol on the trip. But they ran out of their supply of dried medicinal herbs, and the arid region didn't get enough rainfall to support growth of the plants needed for his treatments. The elder's health continued to decline.

They're journey had proceeded fairly smoothly until one afternoon riders, coming from three different directions, converged on the unsuspecting travelers. The motley gang of scruffy outlaws included two white men, two Hispanics and one Native. The white men brandished the same type of revolver Henry carried. Each of the two Hispanics had an old Mexican pistol. The Native outlaw held a U.S. military style rifle.

Hollering wildly and firing their guns into the air, the outlaws expected the defenseless travelers to freeze in place, cowering in fear for their lives.

What they found instead was a well-prepared group fully capable of defending themselves. In a rehearsed set of moves, Alapay and family hid behind their horses and pulled out concealed weapons that included bows and arrows and firearms. Taya, Kai-ina and Yol quickly took cover beneath the wagon. Alapay and Malik grabbed their bows while Kilik took up a position near the wagon. He pulled out his sling and loaded a musket ball in its small deerskin pouch. Henry flashed his revolver.

For a long moment, no one made a move other than to nock an arrow or cock a pistol.

"You have a choice to make," the tallest white man said. "You can live or die. It's up to you."

He paused, waiting for a reply. None came.

"To live, all you have to do is leave the wagon, the horses and your valuables right where they are and walk away," he continued. "Otherwise, in about ten seconds, you will die."

He smiled an evil smile that revealed mouth full of brown, broken and missing teeth.

Still, no one moved or spoke.

Of course, Henry and Alapay were the only ones who understood what the outlaw was saying. The others, however, understood his intent. After a few moments, Alapay could no longer stand the tension. From her partially hidden place between two horses, she quietly drew back her bow string. Tired of waiting, she stood up, aimed at the man doing the talking and released the arrow.

Before any of the outlaws knew what was happening, the arrow pierced the outlaw. The target uttered a choked grunt and fell from his horse. That action was immediately followed by a volley of bullets, arrows and musket balls. Kilik's musket ball hit the Native, knocking him out cold. He fell to the ground. Several of Henry's revolver bullets found their marks, the other white man and one of the Mexicans.

Unfortunately, a stray bullet struck Henry's

packhorse, Clark. The animal squealed in pain as it collapsed. Lewis, the horse Henry was on, looked back to see his old friend lying there in pain. Henry dismounted and ran to Clark. Lewis followed. The downed steed had been hit in the shoulder, and Henry realized he could do nothing for the animal but put him out of his misery.

"Easy, boy," the man said as he aimed his revolver at a spot between Clark's ears.

Meanwhile, the other Mexican had turned his horse and began galloping away. Malik's arrow hit the escaping outlaw, and he slumped forward in his saddle as the animal sped on into the distance.

All was quiet for a few moments except for the receding sound of hoofbeats. Then a moan came from the outlaw Indian. Alapay immediately nocked another arrow and ran to the man. His eyes were fluttering open.

Standing over him, she drew her bow and said, "Brother, you picked the wrong side."

His eyes flared wide open as he realized what was happening.

"You have about two heartbeats to get on your horse, ride out of here and never look back," she added.

Without a word, the man rose from the ground holding the wound in his side, mounted his horse and rode away. Turning back to her family, Alapay found them all staring at her.

"What?" she said. "He would've killed us if he could."

"You're right," Malik said. "I just didn't think you had it in you."

"Now you know better, cousin," she replied as she slung the bow over her shoulder.

"Anybody hurt?" Henry called out in Spanish after he finished saying farewell to his trusty companion Clark.

The women emerged from beneath the wagon as Henry gave Alapay a long hug and a kiss on her forehead. Solomol waved weakly from inside the wagon. "I am all right."

Satisfied that no one was injured, Henry said, "Let's gather anything useful from these guys—weapons, ammunition, food, clothing."

Henry moved his things from Clark to Solomol's wagon as the family gathered what they needed.

"We survived this attack because of planning and practice," Kilik offered. "Keep vigilant. This may not be the last time bandits attack."

Chapter 16 – The Place of River Turtles

As they continued south, Kai-ina began seeing landmarks she recognized from her early days among her Yokuts people. That evening when they stopped to camp for the night, she talked to Kilik about it.

"We are moving through an area my people used to travel through," she told her husband. "Soon we'll come to the Kaweah River, which runs into Tulare Lake. We can get fresh water there and possibly find deer, elk and fish to eat."

"And a bath," Alapa remarked, overhearing their conversation.

"And a bath," Kai-ina agreed.

Traditionally, California Natives, particularly the Chumash, often lived near bodies of water. In addition to being sources of food, the rivers, lakes and streams provided a means of bathing. In some cases, Natives took baths in those bodies of water. In other cases, they took sweat baths inside village sweat houses that used water from those nearby water sources.

Following her directions, the group made its way to the lake, and what a beautiful sight it was. Flocks of birds circled above the water, searching for fish to eat. Deer and elk gathered at the lake's marshy edges to drink.

"The Yokuts people from many villages used to hunt and fish here," Kai-ina said. "But they stopped several years ago because of the growing number of strangers and the decrease in game animals."

After refreshing themselves in the lake and having a meal of fish, the travelers pressed on. Again, following Kai-ina's directions, their odyssey continued past the lake in a southwest direction. The wide-open Central California Valley was home to vast grasslands and roaming herds of elk, deer and antelope.

Kai-ina's guidance across this valley proved invaluable. Thanks to her father's instructions, Kilik's wife was able to guide them toward a break in the coastal mountain range. Following a zig-zag pattern of passes, they crossed the Inner Coastal Mountains and followed a creek down the western slopes.

As they descended into another valley, they could see a set of crumbling buildings in the distance. Continuing along the creek, they came to the ruins of a Spanish mission. Malik scouted ahead on horseback to see if it was safe to approach the place.

Upon closer inspection, he found that the structures were indeed crumbling and appeared vacant. Hearing hoofbeats, an elderly padre emerged from one of the buildings that still stood. After a brief conversation with the man, Malik returned to his family.

"This is, or was, Mission San Luis Obispo," Malik reported. "The priest there offered to rent us a couple of rooms for the night, if we wanted to stay."

"I wouldn't set foot in that place if you paid me," Kilik said defiantly.

"Neither would I," his father echoed weakly.

"If this is the San Luis Obispo mission, that means we're in the northern part of Chumash territory!" Tuhuy said with excitement. "We're maybe three days from home."

That news brightened everyone's spirits.

In another two days, the group reached what was once a Chumash village site named Lompoc. Tuhuy knew that another Spanish mission was located nearby. Soon they came to Mission La Purisima Concepcion, which was another set of crumbling ruins.

"I wonder if all the missions look like this now,' Tuhuy said. "Piles of dissolving adobe bricks."

"I hope so," Yol said, voicing the thoughts of the rest of the family.

They camped near a creek just outside the mission grounds for the night. Next morning, the weary group followed a wagon trail heading east. A small faded sign printed in Spanish said the next mission was eighteen miles.

At around noon, the ten travelers came upon another set of abandoned ruins. The four who'd lived in this mission had been wondering how they'd react if and when they ever saw the place again. Here, now fifty-years later, the original layout was still visible though the dilapidated old walls were only a jagged reminder of the past.

"Take me closer," Solomol said as he weakly sat up in the wagon. "I need to go inside those ravaged walls."

The caravan slowly moved closer. In spite of his feeble condition, Solomol climbed out of the wagon with his son's help, and the two walked toward the mission cemetery.

Passing by the decrepit, unhinged gate and the headstones reserved for Catholic priests, the pair moved to the rear of the graveyard.

"Hundreds of our Chumash people are buried in an unmarked trench back here," Solomol said. "Their death was noted in the mission records. Then their bodies were dumped, and dirt thrown over them. I'd like to offer a traditional Samala blessing song, if I can still remember it."

Kilik stood next to his father, supporting the elder, as he began his song. Solomol's voice was raspy yet filled with dignity. It wasn't long before the rest of the party joined them at that sacred spot. Remembering a little of the song, Yol began to sing, as well.

In that moment, a small bit of healing began—an emotional healing shared by the members of this one little group of Native survivors. Henry tried to imagine how Alapay and her family were feeling right then. He'd only heard a few stories about the harsh mission days in Spanish California. Solomol, Yol, Kilik and Tuhuy had lived it.

After the song ended, Solomol insisted on making his way into the mission courtyard, once the center of his and Yol's daily life. The two elders stood in the center together.

"It does my heart good to see this place in ruins," Solomol told Yol. "We outlasted them, didn't we, Yol?"

"Not only did we outlast them," she replied. "We have children and grandchildren who can pass down a little of what life was like before the strangers came and share the true stories of mission life with future generations."

After spending another quiet moment surrounded by the rubble, Solomol said, "Please take me to the Place of River Turtles now. I've waited long enough."

Kilik helped his father back into the wagon, noticing that the old man felt hot to the touch.

"He has a fever," Kilik whispered to his cousin. "I think he's getting worse."

"I'll look for the appropriate herb when we get to the old village site to make a medicinal tea for him," Tuhuy said.

The trail continued on for another few miles, but it was only about three miles to the Indian settlement Alapay had seen through the Eyes of the Condor. Off to their right, down the hill and near a creek sat a few dwellings made of trees and branches that had been lashed together. They looked nothing like the half-dome tule reed houses that Chumash people traditionally made.

Leaving everyone else near the wagon, Alapay and Malik went down the hill to check out the situation. They saw a Native family just putting the finishing touches on their home.

Alapay called, "Haku, Haku!" using the traditional Chumash greeting.

"Haku!" the father of the family called back.

Alapay was excited to hear that word spoken back. She continued speaking in Samala.

"We have come such a long way from up north to return to this family's original home," she said as she and Malik walked closer.

"Lo siento, no entiendo," the man said, speaking Spanish. "Sorry, I don't understand. We only know one word of Chumash."

"I didn't expect that," Alapay said to Malik in Samala as they just looked at each other.

The cousins switched to Spanish to explain who they were, where they'd come from and what they hoped to do. In turn, the Native man described recent events that had led to them moving to this location.

"After many years, church leaders finally gave us back this piece of land to live on," the man, whose name was Alfonso, told them.

"Most of us here are Chumash. A few others who also lived in the same mission, are from other tribes. None of us speaks our Native language any longer. There may be one person here who speaks some Chumash."

The cousins chatted with the man for a short while. Then Alapy thanked him for the information, and the cousins returned to the wagon.

"The Place of River Turtles is not too far upstream from here," Solomol said between coughs. "Let's keep going."

Up and over a couple of rolling hills the travelers went until Kilik spotted a faintly familiar-looking knoll. After reaching that overlook, his eyes followed the slope down to the river. There sat that rounded finger of land he remembered, surrounded by water on three sides: The Place of River Turtles.

Solomol could no longer stand on his own so Kilik and Tuhuy helped the elder out of the wagon and down the slope.

"Look, Father," Kilik said joyfully. "There it is below us, our old home site."

Solomol managed a brief smile as he repeatedly pointed a crooked finger down the hill.

"Take me down there," he said. "That's where I want to be."

The others followed behind as Kilik and Tuhuy carried the elder between them in a seated position down the hill. Soon they were standing where their homes once stood. The cousins set Solomol down on the ground, leaning his back against a large tree stump.

Only a few charred posts and circles of stones remained of the once vibrant village. But that didn't matter to any of them. They allowed their bare feet to rest on the earth there. Even Alapay and Malik, who'd never set foot on Chumash soil, scooped up handfuls of the stuff to feel it and smell it.

Too weak to speak loudly, Solomol whispered something to his son.

"My father asks that we all gather around," Kilik said to the others.

Again, Solomol whispered to his son.

"He says the spirits of our ancestors linger here," Kilik said, once everyone had seated themselves nearby. "They are dancing at the water's edge."

Tuhuy placed a hand on his uncle's head and quietly whispered a prayer in Samala.

Feeling a temporary surge of energy, the elder spoke just loud enough for his family to hear him.

"Thank you all for making this journey," Solomol said in a raspy voice. "I'm so proud that you children and grandchildren have never forgotten who you are or where you came from."

The elder was briefly interrupted by a coughing spell. After taking a drink of water, he was able to finish what he wanted to say.

"Finally, we are home, home where we belong—the place where our people come from. May your children and your grandchildren remain here forever."

After that, the elder closed his eyes and rested.

Two days later, Solomol died and was laid to rest at the Place of River Turtles. He was eighty years old. With Alapay's help, Tuhuy performed, as best he could remember, the funeral ceremony in the old Chumash traditional way. Yol was the only member of the family left from her generation, and the younger ones respected and treasured her.

The remaining members of the family began getting to know the thirty-or-so other Native people in the nearby settlement.

Spanish was their primary language, though each knew a few Chumash words. Having lived traumatized lives under Spanish and then Mexican rule, almost everything that made them Native had been replaced by the colonists' culture.

But, some of the old ways <u>did</u> survive. These traditions were practiced in secret, away from the prying eyes of outsiders who might punish Natives for trying to still be Native. If history had taught them anything it was that telling people you were Native could get you killed.

After building simple houses made of building materials scrounged from the surrounding countryside, Kilik and family settled into new daily routines. Hunting, fishing, gardening and gathering filled their days. Stories and songs filled their evenings. Dreams and visions of a brighter future filled their nights.

Using pen, ink and stacks of paper he'd hauled with him all the way from San Francisco, Henry spent several months writing his book about living with California Indians. By the dim light of an oil lamp, he often worked late into the night. From time to time, he'd check with Alapay or one of the other family members about an event he couldn't quite remember or an aspect of Native life he wanted accurately record.

When he finally finished, it was time for him to say goodbye. Alapay always knew this day would come, but it made her very sad none-the-less. For months they lived together, loved each other, and fought side-by-side against common enemies.

"I wish you'd come with me," he told her time and time again.

"My place is here with my people," she had replied to him time and time again.

And so they parted ways. It would take him several days to get to Los Angeles by horse and then four to five months to reach Washington, D.C. by ship.

Six months after Solomol died, a beautiful baby girl was born to Malik and Mariposa. They named her Maria Wonono De La Tierra.

In another six months, Alapay gave birth to a baby boy who was given the name Enrique Manual Salapay Solares. And so, another set of cousins were born to the family, destined to grow, play, learn and live together.

Indeed, generations of Samala Chumash people have continued to survive and even thrive. Once, almost erased from the face of the earth, they still remain in the lands of their ancestors.

The End

Afterward

It is a miracle that any Native Americans survived the events of California history. Wave upon wave of foreigners colonized these indigenous lands, bringing with them prejudices and biases against Native Americans.

Speaking eighty different languages, California Indians had no effective means of uniting to repel the outsiders who possessed superior weapons and had no qualms about using those weapons to subdue the local race.

UCLA professor and historian Benjamin Madley called the destruction of California Indians "genocide" and laid out his argument in painful detail in his book An American Genocide, which is one of the historical sources used as a resource for Lands of our Ancestors.

Those Natives who survived California history were severely traumatized as their cultures, languages, social and family connections, and abilities to parent were decimated. This type of trauma produces people that are unable to function normally, and that dysfunctionality is passed on to succeeding generations. This phenomenon, called historical trauma or intergenerational trauma, effects almost every California Indian alive today.

Many people resort to self-medication in the form of alcohol or drugs in attempts to numb bad feelings created by the trauma.

True healing requires a lot of work that can include substance abuse counseling, domestic violence counseling and family therapy. But relearning tribal cultures and languages, along with participating in traditional Native ceremonies and practices, provide some of the most effective paths to better emotional and mental health.

In the last twenty years or so, many California tribes have been doing just that: reintroducing their own tribal languages and cultural practices to tribal members. Some, such as the language and culture apprentices of the Samala Chumash tribe, have even obtained teaching certificates that allow them to teach tribal language and culture in the state's public classrooms.

Teachers, students and parents can and should reach out to local tribes to learn more about those peoples and their cultures who have lived on the lands of their ancestors for ten thousand years or more.

Bibliography of Research Sources

1. Madley Benjamin. <u>An American Genocide: The United States and the California Indian Catastrophe</u>. Yale University Press, New Haven, 2016.

2. Miller, Joaquin. <u>Unwritten History: Life Among the Modocs</u>. Orion Press, Eugene, 1972 (First Published 1873).

3. Silliman, Stephen W. <u>Lost Laborers in Colonial California: Native Americans and the Archaeology of Rancho Petaluma.</u> University of Arizona Press, Tucson, 2004.

4. Heizer, Robert F. <u>The Destruction of California Indians</u>. University of Nebraska Press, Lincoln, 1974.

5. Secrest, William B. <u>When the Great Spirit Died: The Destruction of California Indians</u>. Craven Street Books, Fresno, 2003.

6. Richard Applegate and the Santa Ynez Chumash Education Committee. <u>Samala-English Dictionary: A Guide to the Samala Language of the Ineseño Chumash People</u>. Santa Ynez Band of Chumash Indians, Santa Ynez, 2007.

7. Kroeber, A.L. <u>The Yokuts Language of South Central California</u>. University of California Publications.

8. Cook, Sherburne F. <u>The Conflict Between the California Indian and White Civilization</u>. University of California Press, 1976.

9. Hudson, Travis. "Patterns of Chumash Names," <u>The Journal of California Anthropology</u>, pages 259-272, December 1, 1977.

About the Author

Gary Robinson, a writer and filmmaker, has spent more than thirty years working with American Indian communities to tell the historical and contemporary stories of Native peoples in all forms of media.

His television work has aired on PBS, Turner Broadcasting, FNX and other networks. Some of his most recent work can be seen online at Native Flix (www.nativeflix.com). His non-fiction books, <u>From Warriors to Soldiers</u> and <u>The Language of Victory</u>, have revealed little-known aspects of American Indian service in the U.S. military from the Revolutionary War to modern times.

He is also the author of eight short novels in the *PathFinders* series published by 7th Generation/Native Voices Books. This unique series of books features Native American teen main characters who go on adventures and rediscover the value of their own tribal identities. (www.NativeVoicesBooks.com)

His children's books include <u>Native American Night Before Christmas</u> published by 7th Generation/Native Voices Books.

All his books are available on Amazon.com.

He lives in rural central California. More information about the author can be found at www.garyrobinsonsauthor.com or www.tribaleyeproductions.com and www.youtube.com/tribaleyepro. Like his page on Facebook at www.facebook.com/tribaleyepro.